Spell/Sword

G. Derek Adams

Copyright © 2013 G. Derek Adams

Cover Illustration: Mike Groves – poopbird.com

Cover Layout and Design: Margaret Poplin

All rights reserved.

ISBN-10:0615782760
ISBN-13: 978-0615782768 (Lodestar)

DEDICATION

To my mother, who always wanted to know about my dreams.

CONTENTS

	Acknowledgments	i
20	Chapters	
4	Villainous Interludes	
2	Main Characters	
1-11	Fight Scenes	[depending on definition]
1	Minotaur	[sadly]
1	Subterranean Dance Scene	
2	Good Parts	
1	Sword named 'Chester'	
1	Witch	

ACKNOWLEDGMENTS

You.

I acknowledge you, the person reading this book right now, that took a chance. You took a CHANCE, you crazy-ass dreamer. You picked up the book with the absurd cover and the silly name and you decided to give it a shot.

For this you are my friend, my employer, my boon companion.

You honor me with your chance taking ways – for the tiny erg of faith it took to pick this book up.

I promise to work to the edge of my ability to prove worthy of that poorly advised and researched faith.

You probably made a poor choice – but I want to make you feel acknowledged.

See you at the end of the book.

ii

Sing in me, O Muse
the tale of two travelers, the ones who burned
across ruddy hill and serpent trail –
the last golden days of youth
before the fall.
Spell and sword,
song and steel-
the green hills roll on, and the dark forest waits
but before the sun dies,
let the thousand tales be told again,
forgotten cradle-rhymes spun again,
glory-gold and terror-black,
the tale of two
before the shadows fall.

1

Jonas pulled his dagger from the ogre's eye.

It smelled like vanilla.

Blood the color of clotted cream jetted across his chest and brow, leaving a shiny residue as it clumped and slid down his face. The giant creature bellowed, petroglyph-fingers tightening. Jonas' neck popped as the ogre flung him through the air --- blind and smelling like a feast-day cupcake.

He landed hard against an old stone wall. A gray stone shaped like a bull's head, dislodged by the impact, rolled languorously from the top of the wall and plunked into his lap. Jonas scooped white eye-blood off his face with one hand, while idly patting his new stone-friend with the other. Distantly, he could hear the shouts of encouragement from the drunken townsfolk and the terrible chest-bellow of the ogre. He was a squire lost from his knight, and this was not his first evening in the mud.

"Hey, Rock,." the squire said, friendly and drunk.

The squire started to sit up, then groaned with pain. He leaned his head back against the wall. It was a beautiful night. The three moons hung stately overhead, and the stars winked at him kindly. Wasn't he supposed to be doing something?

The red-leather boot of the ogre detonated the stone wall, showering Jonas with chipped granite and bits of mortar. He turned his head slightly to the right to get a detailed look at the fine stitching of the footwear. The squire pulled himself up and hefted the cow-stone, the only weapon at hand. Grunting, he brought the stone down sharply on the vast creature's veined knee. All he managed to do was dislodge a few flakes of cracked, dry skin.

"Come on, Rock!" Jonas scolded. "You can do better than that, can't you?"

Jonas scrambled away back into the center of the town's square, tottering slightly. A goat-faced man yelled some crude advice, spewing yellow spittle down into his scraggly gray beard. The ramshackle group of barfolk raised their tankards to the sky and laughed.

Jonas considered joining them. Even though the pain in his back was sharp, everything else was blunted and alcohol-gleam amusing.

The ogre pulled his boot free of the wall and turned. The white eye-blood poured down his pomegranate face, the ruined socket still pulsing. The remaining eye focused on the squire, standing in the center of the village square.

2

Jonas tossed his unreliable stone-friend aside and reached for his dagger.

His hand closed on an empty belt.

Oh yeah, Jonas thought. *Lost that a minute ago.*

He ran towards the ogre, hoping to close the distance. The creature was three times his height and many, many times his strength. His only chance lay in somehow taking advantage of the one wound he'd managed to inflict. *Wish I had my sword, I'd tear this monster apart. As easy as---*

A red-leather boot crunched into the squire's chest, sending him flying again. Jonas landed on his back, breathless. He feebly tried to beat down the ringing in his ears, hoping to at least hear the ogre's approach. A fistful of heartbeats limped past, and he raised his head from the cobblestones to look around.

The ogre was turned slightly away from Jonas, speaking with a blonde man dressed in the brown cloak of a town guard. The red-faced ogre leaned over the man, speaking determinedly and pointing several times in Jonas' direction. A few drops of creamy white rained down as the ogre's face shook in agitation. The guardsman kept his hand on his truncheon and took a step back to avoid the spray. Several drunken locals stood close by, offering assistance and clarification in a subdued and helpful manner.

The ringing in Jonas' ears slowly subsided, and he pulled himself up to a sitting position, palms flat on the cobblestones. His stomach turned, slopping over with ale. Now that the excitement of the battle was wearing off, he felt sick.

The ogre stood frowning, one massive hand clapped over

its ravaged eye. The other men from the inn stood close by, patting the massive creature with hands of solemn commiseration. The brown-cloaked guard swept away from them and made his way toward the battered squire.

"You'll be coming with me, boy,." the guardsman said. "You're under arrest for attacking a citizen without provocation."

Jonas nodded. "Make sure you arrest Rock. He attacked too."

Then the squire vomited up several glasses of poorly fermented ale onto the guardsman's boots.

The guard cast his eyes to the heavens as he pulled free his wooden baton. The wood was old and cracked, stained dark with too much polish.

"Sorry about your boots?" the squire offered, wiping his mouth with the sleeve of his tunic.

Somehow, the guard's blow felt harder than the stone wall or the fall onto the cobblestones. Jonas went black.

The cold granite told Jonas that he was awake again.

He was in a cell. Three stone walls and a door made of iron bars. His ribs were full of dirty glass, and red blood had oozed from a cut he hadn't noticed before at his hairline. Jonas looked down at the floor, where his features had been stamped in drying blood on the granite floor.

A completely average face, with a sharply pointed jaw. A

SPELL/SWORD

square nose and a flat forehead like the side of an anvil. The face of a baker's son. Which made sense, because that's what he was.

If they hadn't checked my sword at the gates, I could've won that fight. His hand scuffed the floor, trying to blot the bloody impression. *And probably be in jail for murder.*

Jonas chuckled, then winced. One of his teeth was twisted oddly. He prodded it with his finger, but it wiggled only slightly.

He felt around the darkened cell and found the wall. To slide his back up against it required only a little pain and nausea. Voices floated from down the hallway, where he spied a slim yellow crack of light and an open doorway.

"Damn fool kid. Every time a caravan hits town this happens."

The voice was gray smoke coming from a dying campfire. A younger, brighter voice answered.

"Yeah, but you have to admit he did quite a number on Sundown Jackson. Cut out his freaking eye! The kid's got some spirit."

"Pfeh," the older voice said.

The two voices were coming closer. Jonas tried to decide whether it would be better to pretend to be asleep but couldn't make up his mind before warm torchlight spilled through the iron bars into his cell.

"Awake, huh?" the first voice said. An older man, thinning white hair kept closely cropped. Jonas recognized the younger man with him as the guard who'd knocked him

5

out.

"Yeah."

"I'm Captain Ruck. You have anything to say for yourself?".

"When do I get fed?" Jonas asked politely.

The younger guard snickered but quickly covered his mouth with a hand. Captain Ruck rolled his eyes and leaned against the bars on one elbow. He looked down at the young man.

"Not your first time in a cell, eh? I think you'll be needing to swallow a bit more water before you think about putting any food down in your stomach." He kicked the bottom of the bars with his foot, drawing Jonas' attention to a small clay jug. The squire pulled himself across the floor towards it.

"Where were you trained, boy?" the captain asked.

Jonas hooked one finger through the handle of the jug and pulled it across the floor. Still belly-down, he tilted the jug forward enough for a few swallows of water to splash across his lips and down his throat. He noticed idly that the excess didn't quite erase the red stamp his face had made on the floor.

"Oh, I wasn't trained," Jonas said. "Just a natural, I guess."

"Boy. Look at me," Ruck said.

The squire pulled his eyes from the floor, and looked across the cell. The captain's eyes were firm.

SPELL/SWORD

"Lying doesn't suit you. Now listen close. You've done something very stupid. You are in a strange town, where no one will speak for you. I don't know where you came from, but in this town a little courtesy isn't such a bad thing." The old man grunted, and Jonas felt the first tickles of guilt making their way through the sour ale in his stomach. "I think you're still fairly drunk. We'll talk more in the morning. Most likely you'll be whipped and turned out at the gates, but that'll take a day or two for the magister to pass sentence. We can make your stay very uncomfortable if needs be. Think on it."

Jonas let his head drop. The captain seemed like a decent man. He wanted to tell him where he was from, where he'd been trained. But that would only lead to more questions, questions he didn't have the answer to. Better to keep his mouth shut.

Ruck sighed and turned to leave. The younger guard leaned for a moment against the cell door, waiting for the captain to exit. As the outer door swung shut, Jonas saw the man's hands go to the front of his leggings. A bright stream of urine hit the floor, mingling with the blood and water-- the red stamp of his face.

"Yeah, think on it. Think, think, think." The guard left, whistling a merry tune.

Jonas laid down, as far from the yellow puddle as he could manage. This was his life now, his life on the weary road. He'd been running for months and this was far from the worst day. Nothing to be done about it, just get some sleep and hope that tomorrow there would be a brighter road for him to follow.

Master always said that. The squire drifted to sleep, and

7

thought about the knight he'd left behind.

Captain Ruck sat at his desk and pressed thick fingers to his forehead. His headaches were an old friend, stopping by most days in the late afternoon. Tap, tap they knocked on his head and settled in for a long evening chat.

That's when the drinking started. He did have a guest, after all.

But lately, his painful visitor had taken to visiting earlier and earlier, sometimes around lunch, sometimes before he'd finished his second cup of coffee. Here it was, a bare two hours after dawn and he could hear his guest's feet coming up the path.

Keeping the pressure on his forehead with one hand, Ruck groped for the steel bottle in his bottom drawer. The metal was cool on his lips as he drank deep.

Bronberry leaned into the room and smiled a toothy grin.

"Taking lunch a little early, Captain?"

"Shut your mouth, Bronberry. I'm in no mood." Ruck stoppered the bottle and slammed it back into the drawer.

His lieutenant was a handsome sort. Blonde and lean, nice clean hands. Ruck hated him.

"I think that boy in Cell Three is finally coming around. He hasn't puked in a couple of hours, I figure. Want me to drag him down for sentencing? Or do you need a few more...minutes?" The young guard smiled and drawled out

SPELL/SWORD

the last word.

Ruck's stomach tightened with bile. He took a few short breaths.

"Bring him down, Bronberry. Now," he replied.

The young guard saluted with a careless hand and slid from view.

Ruck slid his thick fingers through thinning hair and tried to keep from immediately taking another long drink from the bottle. He failed, but managed to have the steel bottle safely back in its place before Bronberry returned with the prisoner.

Bronberry pushed the boy roughly onto the wooden bench and bolted his manacles to the old iron ring. The guard slapped the back of the boy's head and nodded to the captain.

"He's all yours, Captain. Have fun!" The door shut briskly.

The boy's skin was pale, and he looked absurdly hungover. He looked around the room, disheveled mop of curly brown hair matted to his skull. *He's so young,* Ruck thought. *Can't be more than fifteen.*

"How are you feeling, boy?" Ruck asked.

The prisoner said nothing.

The captain rolled his eyes and rubbed his forehead for a moment. He stood and leaned forward. Ruck grabbed his guard's baton from the corner of his desk and thumped the young man squarely on his shoulder.

9

"Ow!" the boy said.

"Paying attention now? Maybe you don't remember from last night -- and with the amount you drank, I wouldn't be surprised -- but it's time to start cooperating. Answering questions, doing as you're told, and if you don't start right now, I'm going to loosen your tongue with this."

The boy furrowed his brow and stared at the baton for a long moment. He shrugged.

"I feel fine..." The truncheon rose slightly. "...Sir. I feel fine, sir."

"And what's your name?"

"Jonas of... Jonas. Jonas is my name."

Ruck poked the boy's shoulder again. "Good. I don't care where you're from; Jonas will do. Now, do you remember fighting with Sundown Jackson, the ogre?"

"I think my children will remember it."

"You got very drunk, and then some friendly men asked you if you'd like to make some money. A quick fight for some quick gold. Am I right so far?"

The boy looked at Ruck with surprise, then nodded.

"They led you around the back of the Oak, and they started betting. A copper, two silvers -- why not some gold? This boy looks sharp! Hey, friend, you want to bet on yourself? Oh, only a few coppers? Well, I'll hold it for you, and give you a silver for every copper if you win!" Ruck tapped the baton against his cheek as his voice grew bored. "And, surprise, ogre. Right?"

SPELL/SWORD

Jonas rolled his head back and cut his eyes towards the window.

"What I don't get," Ruck continued, "is why didn't you run? Most travelers do, at that point."

The boy lolled his head forward for a moment, hair falling across his face.

"Figured I could win, I guess," The boy said seriously.

2

Rime watched the man burn.

The left ear held out the longest, oddly pink and vibrant amidst the flames. It melted like candle wax. She concentrated and increased the heat, pouring fire down until the pork-fat-popping corpse shuddered and laid still. The fire coiled back inside her, and she noticed the sudden quiet, absent of screams. The campsite stank of burning.

She was going to need a new butler.

Pushing her hair out of her eyes, Rime stepped back into her wagon to think. The eyes of her driver and the other two caravan guards followed like frightened rabbits. "Mage..." one whispered in shock.

They would leave as soon as dark fell, she knew. Slipping between trees and risking a broken horse leg in the hopes of escaping her. A little bit braver, or further from civilization, they might have risked attacking her, and stealing the tidy chest of gold she kept under her bunk. She had chosen this exact moment to burn Murphy, right where the caravan guards could see. Hopefully it would

SPELL/SWORD

buy her enough time to recover.

The spell-pain took her as soon as she closed the door to her wagon. A tremendous nausea in her gut and a throbbing in her temples. Blurred vision was inconvenient, so she closed her eyes to focus. Rime made herself move her feet slowly, feeling for the edge of the chair, of the desk, then finally her bunk. The girl slid on top of the blanket as the world spun.

Murphy had deserved it. The wizened old man her father had sent as guide, advisor, and manservant had been solicitous enough, when he wasn't drinking with the guards or falling off his horse. A little too familiar at times, running his spider hands over her shoulders down to the small of her back. She had tolerated it as a necessary evil.

Then she had found the note.

A scribbled letter from someone, promising gold in return for her route. For making sure the guards were properly drunk on the night of the next Full White. Rime had folded the note precisely four times after reading it.

She had stood over his pack for several moments after that, the drunken butler's few possessions spilled on the ground as he snored next to the campfire. It was an hour before dark, but he had been drunk since lunch. Her steps were precise as she crossed the distance and laid the paper in his hands. A few prods with her boot had woken him, and the look in his eyes as he pawed the note open was all that she needed.

Rime laid in her bed, the world spun, and she watched the man burn again and again as she fell into darkness.

She awoke, sweat-damp hair sticking to her face.

It was dark outside; a few hours had passed. Rime rose and moved to open her wagon's door.

They'd taken the horses, as expected. Only the two hitched to her wagon remained. She nodded in satisfaction. Fear had aided her.

The fire cast dying light around the clearing. A steel pot lay in the embers, charring on one side. She could smell burning beans, and a stranger odor. *Burning butler.*

The pile of wood the driver and caravan guards had gathered remained. Rime tossed a few logs onto the fire and sat down to think. Her driver had always fussed over the fire, making certain that the logs were laid in an exact pattern. She noted that wood burned, regardless of how it was laid. This was the first fire she had ever tended.

The slim girl sat down on a stone and stared into the flames.

Before stealing off into the night, the hired men had the forethought to take Murphy's charred body with them. It would lend credence to any tale they might tell. She had no range-craft, but she assumed they would make haste back the way they had come, back to their homes in the city of Carroway. They had no business down this road anymore.

I wonder if they read the note? I wonder if they know I saved their lives?

Rime thought back to Murphy's death. The note had probably burned.

The girl flicked her hand in a gesture of dismissal.

By the extremely accurate map her father had kept on his study wall, she was no more than a day's travel from Talbot. Beyond that the canyons. Beyond that, what she needed. Gold would buy more men in Talbot, enough to handle whatever forces were waiting when the White Moon was full.

Rime looked at the three moons. The Black Moon was waning, and the Red Moon was a bare sliver on the horizon's rim. The White Moon hung fat in the sky. *Two days.* The girl rubbed her lip. *That's how long I have before I need new guards.* Rime hated the need.

She grabbed a stick and pulled the bean pot out of the fire. The stench was growing tiresome. The clean, steel lid was nearby. Rime saw a brown smear down her face reflected as she put the lid back on. Another nosebleed.

Her guards had stolen all the food, but she still had a water cask slung on the back of her wagon. She scrubbed the dried blood off her face and took a swallow of the stale water, forcing it down.

Rime threw some more logs on the fire, until the clearing filled with light. She was in no mood or condition to deal with any wandering creatures. Her magic was ready, but her body was still used up.

She locked the door to her wagon and laid down on the bed. The girl closed her eyes, willing herself to sleep.

At dawn, she would need to teach herself how to drive the

wagon.

3

The shovel bit into the earth with a satisfying *chaff* sound. Jonas dumped another spadeful of earth in the growing pile to his right. The ditch extended behind him and continued to progress forward at a steady rate. The squire angled the shovel slightly to keep the line straight. *Chaff.* He was completely content. *Chaff.* More dirt on the pile.

Captain Ruck had set him to work.

"From there to there. Three feet deep, four feet wide. Dig." The gray-haired man had tossed a shovel into his prisoner's hands and stomped back into the guardhouse. Jonas saw that he was extending an irrigation line that led to a struggling field behind the building. Wilting corn, desert beans, and some pathetic potatoes.

Jonas had no imagination. His interests extended no further than the reach of his arms. One teacher had said, "There is a flat place in your head, young man. And everything I try to put in there just beads and rolls off."

17

Chaff. More dirt on the pile.

History bored him, and theology put him to sleep. The other squires would talk for hours, having philosophical jousts. Jonas would leave and go work in the yard on his sword forms. Something that mattered.

Chaff. More dirt on the pile. His calloused hands were in no danger of blisters. He was a simple machine given a simple task.

He worked for a few hours, only stopping once or twice to drink from the nearby well. His world had shrunk down to an empty field, a shovel and a line. Jonas felt satisfied. Escape never occurred to him.

A small wagon entered the yard. A pair of expensive horses pulled it, with new tack. The wagon itself was of simple wood but expertly crafted. Jonas eyed the brass fittings around the window and door, and estimated they were worth three times as much as the horses.

A girl drove the wagon, reins wrapped oddly around her hands. She guided the horses to the entrance of the guardhouse, and pulled back sharply to stop the team. Jonas watched her begin to unwind the reins. Her age was hard to place; she was small and thin, but her sharp face seemed far too serious and focused to belong to a child. She looked directly at him.

The squire coughed, and started digging again. Eyes firmly on the ground until the girl walked inside. He heard the door of the guardhouse close and he finally risked looking back up.

Like looking at a snake. Jonas put his foot on the spade once more. *Or...*

The squire had seen that sort of look before, but only on the battlefield. So strange to find the hollow wind of war in the eyes of such a young woman.

Ruck took a long swig from his canteen. He looked at his visitor and took another swallow. An even longer one.

Only then did he say, "Now, what did you say you needed again?"

The girl's eyes bored into his.

"Four guards. A guide to lead me through the Drift Canyons. Also, provisions and supplies for two weeks. I expect to be attacked when I exit the canyons, so the men will need to be highly trained, not drunkards. Do you have anyone like that? At all?"

Ruck considered taking another drink but decided it probably would be undignified.

The girl continued, "I have gold, of course. Half now, half when I am safely returned to Carroway. It should be simple for anyone of reasonable--"

The gray-haired captain raised his hands, and the girl stopped. Ruck rubbed his eyes with the tips of his fingers as he spoke.

"What was your name again?"

"Rime Korvanus. My family is a distinguished House in--"

"Yes, yes, I'm sure they are." The captain rose from his chair. He placed a firm knuckle in the small of his back and stretched.

"Now, young lady. This town is called Talbot. Tell me what you've heard about us."

The girl looked down at the floor, her brows tightening with concentration.

"Talbot. Founded in 1099, by Ezerus Talbot. Miner and prospector. Short-lived vein of silver, led to quick increase of population. Vein depleted 1101. No major exports. Talbot sits in the northern third of the country of Carroway, controlled by a city-state of the same name. The eastern part of the continent of Tel, the second largest land mass in Aufero. Population approximately 3000 as of last census. 90% Human, 5 % Elven, 3% Interracial. 2% Other."

Her voice was clear and precise. Ruck took another drink. Dignity be damned.

The empty canteen clanked against the desk. He took the girl's elbow, completely missing the dangerous look she shot him. Ruck led her swiftly down the hall, past the speculative looks of his useless lieutenant, and back out the front door.

"Talbot is a dying town. There's no warriors here worth a damn, except me and Bronberry, and we aren't riding off any time soon. I suggest you get back on your wagon and--" Ruck stopped as they came out onto the front steps.

The prisoner had unhitched the horses from the wagon and was rubbing them down with a rough, brown cloth. He finished and led them calmly towards the watering

SPELL/SWORD

trough next to the stables. Bronberry stepped out the door behind the captain and the girl.

"Who told you to do that?" Ruck demanded.

"They've had a hard road. They needed to be seen to," Jonas replied.

"Boy," the girl said. "Hitch my horses back up, now."

She pulled her elbow from the captain's nerveless grasp. She inclined her head slightly, minding her manners.

"Good day, Captain." The young girl climbed back into the driver's seat.

The prisoner didn't move. "You'll hurt them if you ride them now. At least let them drink their fill."

Rime turned her head and looked at him.

"Boy. Hitch, my horses back up, now." she said.

Bronberry slid past the captain and came into the yard.

"Come now, Madame... Rime? I hate to admit it, but the prisoner is right. Allow me to escort you to the Oak. It's a fine inn, and you can collect yourself."

Rime leveled a raptor-look. A pitiless, empty stare that gives no glimpse into the mind of the hawk as it dives upon something small and squeaking. Bronberry quailed beneath it, but still managed to lay his hands on the side of the wagon and spread a toothy smile as a final barricade.

Rime closed her eyes for a moment.

21

"Fine. Show me."

The prisoner led the horses to the water trough, where their grateful necks bowed.

The smell of roasting potatoes and burnt mutton filled the warm confines of The Oak. The tables were mostly empty, only a few old men leaning on the bar. A battered jukebox gave off a weak green glow and scratched music in equal measure. The girl cocked an eyebrow at the device, surprised to find a powered device this far from civilization. Her father's manor in Valeria bristled with energy and automation, chrome and burn-light glass carefully maintained by the household staff. This sad device seemed barely functional, the electric eel that powered it poorly fed and sickly, its head buried in the far corner of the dirty aquarium at the jukebox's base. The music dipped and slid in tempo and volume, staggering forward as the jukebox and the eel waited for death.

That'll be the way,
your eyes will burn
and that'll be the way
your love will turn
and that'll be the way,
that I find my way into your
memory of love
memory of love
memory of looooooove

Rime scanned the room slowly, taking in the large brick fireplace fashioned to look like the roots of a giant tree. A gap-toothed graybeard leaned away from the bar to stare.

SPELL/SWORD

He craned his head so far back that the battered yellow hat he wore flopped onto the cedar-wood floor. The blonde guard swept past her and leaned over the bar, shouting towards the back where steam rose above short black curtains stamped with oak leaves.

"Two ales, Varilla. A hog sandwich for me, and... What'll you take, little miss?" Bronberry gestured in Rime's direction with slime-coated chivalry.

She walked to the first table available and sat down.

Keeping his over-solicitous gaze on her, he continued. "Just the sandwich, Varilla -- maybe a muffin?"

Rime shook her head.

"Bring the muffin, Varilla!"

She folded her hands together. Her sense of doubt was growing with each moment spent in the fool's company. Rime watched as the guard took his sweet time glad-handing the old men at the bar, helping himself to a stick of licorice from a large dirty jar on the counter.

Rime went to her library.

She closed her eyes, then opened them.

Her eyes were now windows, through them the dirty bar and the prating guard. Inside her head, she sat on a white stool with a thick leather cushion. A book was in her hands, still open to the page that listed the paltry information about Talbot which she had befuddled the drunken captain with. And all around her, tall shelves filled with books.

23

Books about ships and how to tie knots. A book about jam-making next to a book about siege tactics. A book of poetry, a book of trade law, a book of Yad-Elf songs and Nai-Elf riddles. Books on carpentry, books on the proper forms of etiquette in the court of Gilead, books on the forgotten philosophies of the Eight Shattered Dwarven Monasteries.

History books. Botany texts. Lexicons and dictionaries by the score. Neat, tidy rows on the clean, white shelves of her mind. Every book she had ever read, kept perfect and complete here in her library. All of the knowledge in her father's collection and every tome she had managed to beg or borrow from visiting scholars. There were even a few that her tutor had shared, but they were stitched up with leather and bone, and Rime kept those on a back shelf, only using them if she had no other choice.

The walls of knowledge comforted her, calmed her. They were organized in a labyrinthine system of staggering complexity, using a combination of tertiary logic sequences and the rhyme scheme of a hymn written in a dead language. That Rime's favorites were closest to the window was merely a coincidence, or so she often reassured herself.

And her favorites were the books of numbers.

She put the drab travelogue back in its place and opened an algebra book to let her friends out.

They shook free at once, glowing incandescent green. Fives and sevens waltzed through the air while twos and nines squabbled under a tree with parabolic arcs for leaves and a bored-looking eight as the trunk. The green numbers filled the air, their voices a quiet vibration. The numbers never failed her. Rime spread her hands wide feeling the familiar not-heat of their presence. *If only they could be my guards.*

She glanced out through her eye-windows. The blonde guard was slapping another man's shoulder, mouth wide as he brayed at some jest. She would need to leave soon and hear the oaf's voice.

But first she would glance at the Book of Hope.

She kept it on a small pedestal close at hand, as she rarely passed a day without turning its pages. The cover was simple gray wood, cut thin and bound with clean white cord. Rime had made it herself, collecting bits of lore and odd scraps of rumor from many of the other books in her library. It was her prize, her great work. The reason why she traveled now in such haste.

Rime opened the cover and scanned the first few paragraphs. She had been eleven when she began it, and some of the prose wrinkled her nose in embarrassment. The glowing numbers flocked close with interest.

...must, like me, be tied to the 'Magic Wild'. The stories from Eridia and the Sarmad suggest that she is gifted with power beyond the conception of the wizards of Valeria...

"I'll find her. She has to be there," she said, her own words firm and reassuring.

Rime closed the Book. She came to her library often, and read the Book of Hope every time. But there was one thing she almost never did.

Look beyond her library, to the other parts of her mind.

She looked beyond the tidy shelves, and the green number

light into the vast Dark. The dark of her mind. Things moved in the shadows, writhing and growing. Moving and *whispering.*

The more she used her magic, the closer they came. The power was so sweet but in the throes of spell-pain she could begin to see more and more of the shapes in the dark. Dragons. Madness.

Not yet. Rime pressed her fingers into the Book. *Not ever. I'm going to find her.*

She left her library. She blinked, and her eyes refocused on the dirty inn table.

"So, how much gold are we talking?" Bronberry slid into a chair next to her, instead of keeping a proper distance across the table. He pushed a thick blue plate close bearing a titanic muffin, oozing raisins and pride.

"Your captain said you had duties here in town, correct?"

"Well, there's duties... and then there's duties." His broad grin flashed. "How much gold?"

Rime spoke a number very slowly and distinctly. Then she repeated it to ensure that the guard understood her.

Bronberry's eyes widened, and his grin dissolved.

"And twice that when we return, if you can find one more guard, Lieutenant Bronberry."

"I'll find someone, don't you worry," the blonde man choked out. "Boss?"

SPELL/SWORD

He waved to the bartender. Rime smiled, and stood to leave.

"Mistress will be fine."

That'll be the way, Yes that'll be the way... The jukebox spooled on.

"Come on, let me take him." Bronberry said, standing in the captain's doorway.

Ruck had refilled his canteen several times. An angry kettle of alcohol burbled in his belly. The captain glowered at his lieutenant.

"You're running off into the wilderness like a damn fool, abandoning your post! And you want me to not fire you, not throw you in the cells, and let you take a prisoner with you? Well, that's some fine icing on a shitty, shitty cake."

Bronberry leaned forward, fingertips pressing down on the top of Ruck's desk. The younger man's face was sweaty and naked with desire. His words came out in a fierce whisper, even though the two constables were completely alone.

"It's more money than you and I make in five years, old man. You may have pissed away your senses, but not me. The kid's the only one around here who's halfway decent in a fight, and I can collect his wages and give them to you, you ass. Just stamp the papers, and make this his sentence."

Ruck groped around his brain for a sense of duty, but it

slipped through his addled fingers.

The blonde guard smiled and pushed the stamp across the desk.

"Get up, prisoner."

Bronberry leered through the iron bars, a wooden bucket in his hands. Jonas sighed and stood up.

"Your sentence has been decided. You're going to be under my custody, and we're going on a little trip. But first, a bath." The guard swung the bucket back, then flung its contents full into the squire's face. In the small cell he had no way to avoid it. "Can't have you offending the young lady."

Jonas pushed wet hair out of his eyes and flicked water droplets onto the floor.

"Are we going with that girl?" he said. "I'll need my sword."

The blonde guard pushed his face against the bars.

"Just remember that I'm watching you. If you try to run, I'll kill you." He smiled.

"Right," Jonas replied.

The door swung open.

THE KNIGHT OF DUST

The light was dim. A single candle flickered over stacks of old scrolls and tomes and one book opened wide on a battered desk. An old man with gray hair leaned over the pages, silver spectacles perched on his nose, breathing in the smell of story. A hard heel of cheese sat forgotten on a brown plate at his elbow, next to a stone cold cup of tea. The man held the tiny cheese knife in his left hand, absently tapping it against his temple while he read. Tiny particles of dried cheese dotted his brow.

Linus leaned forward eagerly as the lances crashed across the pages. The fair damsel tossed a blue rose to her champion, the thunder of hooves, the creak of the armor. The room was dark, but he sat in the sun. He gasped as the Black Knight rode onto the field. Linus pulled the wool blanket closer around his shoulders eagerly. A flash at the window, a rumble of distant thunder. Linus blinked across the dark room, but the weight of the story pulled him right back in.

The crowd was still and silent, too intimidated to jeer the dark champion. A young girl was sobbing a few benches down. The Black Knight's charger was coal-midnight, his sword an ebony horror. His shield had the only spot of color, a broad white skull with a filthy leer.

Who could stand against this horrid foe? For the good of the kingdom, for the love of Princess Dawn, for the sake of chivalry?

Linus flipped the faded page, upsetting the lone candle in his excitement. "Dunstan," he whispered. "Good Sir Dunstan!"

The candle flame flickered, then was steady.

The white stallion exploded onto the lists. Sir Dunstan's burnished armor gleamed like the sun, long blond hair falling down the back. He made a quick circuit of the stands, and the people finally found their voice, shouting in excitement and joy. Linus chuckled, his nose a few inches from the page.

"Master Linus."

Sir Dunstan ripped his gleaming sword from its scabbard and held it high. The knight locked eyes with the princess and gave the blade a chaste kiss. Princess Dawn's bosom heaved in terror for her champion.

"Linus."

Linus reached to flip the page, and found a black silk glove holding the page down. He looked up, blinking into the the marble face of a young man. In the candlelight, Linus could make out the rest of his attire; an immaculate black tunic and cloak and a conical cap that sloped forward, surmounted by a single silver bell. Long brown hair framed a serious face.

SPELL/SWORD

The old man sighed, and placed the cheese knife in the center of the book to mark his place. His guest removed his hand as the book closed.

"It's been awhile since I've seen you without your mask, Master Song."

The young man smiled in response. He reached into his cloak and pulled forth a featureless wooden mask with thin slits for eyes and mouth. It clattered slightly as he tossed it onto the desk. White as bone on the dark desk. The black knight's shield. "It's been some time since you have seen me at all, Master Linus."

Linus folded his hands on top of the book and steepled his fingers. He surveyed the mask carefully. "You are not here on Council business."

Song stood very still. "Why am I here?"

A test. Thunder rumbled, a flash of light.

"Something that you want kept quiet, something that would endanger your position, something dangerous, something... personal?" The young man didn't twitch. "Oh... something *very* dangerous, and *very* embarrassing. I guess lover -- though family is also possible."

"Do you really think I would come to your door to clean up a lover's tiff? That I would seek out Linus the Blue... Linus the Magekiller... for something any hired thug could handle?" Song seemed disappointed.

"I'm an old man now," *Damn him. He's right.* "Forgive my foggy conclusions, but why seek me at all? Maybe not a hired thug, but you have ample might at your disposal, Master Song... the Ender? Isn't that the title your acolyte

31

wizards have bestowed upon you?"

The young mage turned away, nearly disappearing in the darkness. Linus was reminded of a much younger boy, standing in much the same way when a knight told him that his mother was dead. Time had changed that weeping boy into a figure of true power, and time had changed the knight into an old man reading alone in the dark.

"My sister... has been a problem since her birth. She is an abomination, a wild mage. A sick joke against the pride and honor of my family. Most of her kind manifest at early puberty -- but she showed us what she was when she was three years old." Song's voice was thin. "Three years old."

The old man felt a pang of sorrow, and the clop of the white charger's hooves grew ever more distant. Sir Dunstan would need to wait.

"We kept her... contained. She was raised by tutors at my father's instruction, treated like she was a person and pampered on my family's estate. The old fool even became fond of her, forgetting what she was and how dangerous her kind are. He allowed her liberties: small trips into Valeria, to the library."

"How old is she?"

"Fourteen. Somehow she convinced my father to allow her free reign, to take a trip. A trip!" Song turned back towards the old man. "She departs from Carroway in two day's time, with a pair of wagons, a manservant, and a few light guards. And all the power of sun and winter and death held lightly in her hands. I want you to find her and kill her."

Linus stood up, sliding his chair back. The thick wool

32

SPELL/SWORD

blanket started to slide off his shoulders, but he clutched it closely. His hip popped loudly in the quiet room.

"Your father..." he began.

"Is an old man who loves his daughter." Song walked over to the table and laid two fingers on top of the wooden mask. "This must be done, and it's past time."

"An accident. In the wilderness. Very sad." The old man brushed a morsel of cheese off his cheek.

"There is a chest in the hall. It has more money than you need. Hire whoever you require, pick up the trail in Carroway. She is immensely powerful, so be cautious and be swift."

"Her name? What does she look like?"

"Small. Short brown hair. She could easily pass for a boy." The wizard seemed satisfied with the old man's query. "Her name is Rime. She is also very clever, don't take her youth for granted. The power she wields..."

"It has been a long time, Song -- but I know how to lead a Hunt." The old man's quiet words made the young wizard pause. Song found it hard to meet the other man's gaze.

"That is why I came to you. That and the weapon you once bore." Song's words were quick, then he looked around the room uncertain. "You do still have it... don't you?"

Linus let the blanket fall to the floor. At his side was a long sword. The hilt was unbroken, featureless white.

"It still has me." Linus replied sadly.

33

The white sword slipped free from its scabbard, smooth as glass. Master Song the Ender, one of the Council of Nine, First Necromancer of Valeria, took two steps back in his haste to get away from the featureless blade.

"It will be done, Song. You have my oath on it. I will leave at dawn. Would you care for some tea before you leave?" Linus put the sword tip down and leaned on it like a cane.

The black-cloak wizard shook his head firmly and stepped forward to retrieve his mask. He turned away and left without another word.

Linus held the sword up again and looked at his right hand. The white sword was light, fiendishly light, but his hand still shook with the strain. He sheathed it and pushed his spectacles up on his head. He pinched his nose and began to order his thoughts.Supplies, quick transportation, his old armor would have to be unearthed from the green trunk at the base of his bed. Then travel and blood.

Linus opened his eyes and peered down at the closed book. It was a very good story, one he'd read several times. Good always won, and the Black Knight was roundly defeated. But could he really be sure, if he left it unfinished this time?

The old man pulled the wool blanket back over his shoulders and settled back in to finish the story.

Thunder rumbled and the candle flickered in the dark room. But Linus stood in the sun and cheered.

4

The sword was good steel. That was what his master always called it, and the way he always thought of it. An unadorned hilt made of brown wood, a simple crossguard. The scabbard was old leather, the cord straps and brass rings leaving decades-old impressions in the surface. Jonas checked the edge out of habit. It was sharp, but he'd still spend an hour honing it when the opportunity presented itself. The original shoulder strap had been lost long before it was given to him, so he'd replaced it with a simple length of red cotton rope.

The squire slid the blade back into the scabbard and heard the familiar click of the crossguard hitting the brass. He smiled for the first time since waking up in the cell. It was good to have his sword.

The hooves of the horses crunched into the gravel road, and the wagon wheels droned. A dirty iron chain connected his horse's saddle to the back of the wagon: Bronberry's insurance.

"We're going into dangerous territory, prisoner. On foot

and alone, you don't have much chance. Better to ride it out with me and the girl. You watch the back, obey any orders I give you, and when we get back, you're a free man," Bronberry had said.

What if I kill you in your sleep? Jonas had thought. *As soon as we're outside of the city limits?*

A bray of laughter came from the the front of the wagon. Somehow the laughter even *sounded* blonde.

Guess he's not too concerned. Jonas swung his sword back over his shoulder.

I may have miscalculated. This man is awful.

The blonde guard had kept up a steady stream of chatter all morning. Gossip, boasting, expansive descriptions of memorable meals and feats of drinking. Rime stared stonily ahead.

"...and that's when I said, 'There's no way you can eat that entire squash, Dooley, it's the size of your head! And it's on fire! And it's alive!' And Dooley said..." Bronberry chattered on.

Rime tuned him out. She had to make do with what she had. This blathering fool, and a simpleton stable boy. *Locked up for drinking and starting a brawl. At least he can fight; all this other one does is talk.*

The mage thought of the road ahead and opened her map. It existed only in her mind, an exact copy of the one in her father's study. She had taken to adding small notes of her

SPELL/SWORD

progress, carefully drawn with bright ink on the faded gray map. They had left Talbot at dawn and wouldn't arrive at the entrance to the canyons until tomorrow. Her map showed a small river running between the town and the canyons. She imagined them setting up camp there and then drew a quick picture of a tent on the north bank.

The blonde guard kept talking, and her drawing became more elaborate. A fanciful purple pennant on the tent, then a small cookfire with a steel kettle shaped like a dragon. Rime was especially proud of the steam coming out of its kettle-mouth. Then she turned her mind's quill to the wagon. She spent quite some time drawing the elaborate curliques on the side door. They were clearly better than the foolish House sigil that was on the real wagon. She had become very fond of the wagon in the past few days, but the Korvanus family crest was an unwelcome reminder of home.

Her mind's hand moved beyond her ink campsite, and hovered over the Canyons. Before she could stop herself, she drew creatures. Creatures with teeth, long and sharp. Claws candle-yellow and eyes flame-red.

"...we had to pull a four-inch splinter out of his jaw, the whole time he keeps trying to whistle *Vallydown, Susannah*." Bronberry's voice crested the wave of her thoughts and dissipated her vision. Rime was relieved, then disgusted with herself for permitting the emotion.

"Hey." A voice from behind the wagon. "Someone's following us."

Rime started to rein in the horses, but Bronberry reached over and swatted the horses' rumps to keep them moving.

"Don't do that. If the kid's right... just keep moving like

everything's normal." The guard nimbly untied the leather thong keeping his axe handle secure on his saddle. Bronberry slowed his horse until he was riding next to Jonas.

Rime's eyebrows knit in frustration. She felt her magic slide and coil in her stomach and forced herself to remain calm. *She* was the master here, not the gibbering guard.

Bronberry's face was skeptical, but he scanned the treeline all the same.

"All right, kid. What'd you think you saw? If you've spooked the girl for no reason--"

"About half a mile past the end of my nose, two riders. One of them didn't cover his shield well enough, and it reflects when they cross a sunny patch," Jonas said, without turning his head.

The forest north of Talbot was mainly evergreens, dense needles forcing their way through the rocky soil. Bronberry peered through the shifting boughs -- and he saw them. The two men were moving steadily, clearly keeping the wagon in view. They were making no attempt to outpace the caravan.

"How long have they been there?"

"I noticed them about fifteen minutes ago, but they've probably been following us since town." Jonas scratched his chin.

The guard's hand tightened on his axe uncertainly. They

had been travelling steadily for at least three hours, so no way they could make a dash back for town. He felt a drop of sweat slide down his neck.

"Ambush?" he asked the prisoner.

"Ambush," Jonas replied. "You're from here. Where are they going to hit us?"

Bronberry screwed up his face. "Nothing between here and the Canyons except open road and trees. A river, but we're hours from that. This road is fairly well travelled and goes almost due north. The only way they're going to be able to slow us up is to chop some trees down and make a barricade. I'm going to unhook your horse, and you'll ride up at the front of the wagon with me. The first sight of the barricade, and we'll dash in and hack our way through."

Jonas scratched his chin. He saw a lot of problems with the plan, but knew that the guard wouldn't listen. And having his horse unchained suited him just fine.

The chain clanked as Bronberry undid it. He wrapped the free end around the prisoner's foot and reattached the lock. Jonas was now effectively tethered to the horse. The guard tucked the key back up his sleeve and grinned.

"I just don't want you getting any ideas."

The barricade was not made of wood.

It was a dinosaur.

A massive four-legged saurian straddled the road, its long

neck stretching forty feet in the air. It idly munched on the top of a pine tree as the caravan crested the hill. Strapped to its back was a rough pavilion made of leather and a dirty black fabric. Three archers stood on the pavilion, arrows nocked. The two riders that had followed them galloped forward to join two other ragged looking men approaching from the side of the road. They slid off their horses with obvious relief and pulled swords pitted with rust from filthy belts made of rope and uncured leather.

A tall man in a long orange robe, holding a violin, stood up from the pavilion. He waved his bow at the approaching caravan and began to play. A merry tune filled the air as the gangly man in orange spun and capered between the archers.

The dinosaur stopped munching and started to bob its head slightly.

Bronberry said, "That's just not fair."

"It doesn't matter." Rime pulled back on the reins to bring the wagon to a sharp halt. "What are you going to do about it?"

"This is a little more than some branches across the road." Jonas said. "It's a nice song, though." *Three archers, four men on foot and this madman with the violin.*

The fiddler stopped dancing and lowered his bow. He was wearing a thick blindfold, made from the same fabric as his robe.

"Ah, I hear your wagon wheels grinding to a halt. Welcome, travelers! We've prepared an entrancing panoply of festivities for you, filled with brutal murder and oodles of pain. You were supposed to be unguarded, little girl.

40

SPELL/SWORD

That was the deal we made with your manservant. It's good that I left nothing to chance." His voice had the unpleasant piping sound of a church organ left to corrode.

Bronberry craned his neck left and right and stared longingly back to the south. His horse took a step to the left, as if sensing the rider's hesitation.

"We just want the girl, so if you feel like making your way back to the vast metropolis to the south, you can leave unmolested," the fiddler called, as if he could see the guard's movement.

"The gold," Rime hissed. "Don't forget."

Jonas was already moving his horse forward, drawing his sword. He stopped a few paces ahead and looked back towards Bronberry.

The blonde guard wiped sweat from his palm and unsheathed his axe. The blade was a full half-circle of black iron, riveted to the haft. Jonas nodded and looked back down the road.

"We've got to get to those archers. Girl, turn the wagon sideways and use it for cover."

"My name is Rime," she replied. "And don't..."

"I'm bored!" sawed the blind fiddler, strings screeching. "Kill the guards and bring me the girl."

Three arrows flew, one thudding into the wood above the mage's head. Jonas locked eyes with her for a moment. The bow scratched across the fiddle, and a topsy-turvy tune spooled across the open air.

41

"Rime, then. Do it, please." The squire's voice was absent, his attention on the bandits. He kicked his horse forward

Bronberry swore and followed him, choking up on the axe handle. The young mage blinked and snapped the reins pulling the wagon sharply to the left.

Hooves thudded into the loose gravel of the road. The four bandits on the ground were unmounted -- a small advantage -- but the archers were easily twenty-five feet in the air. *An entrenched position.* Jonas hunched down in the saddle, hoping to be a smaller target. *Got to close the distance fast.*

The squire closed with the first bandit as the bows twanged again. He leaned down as far as he could and slashed at the man. The blade cut deeply into the man's piggish face, and he fell dropping his weapon. The arrows made a shallow *piff* sound as they hit the ground nearby.

The fiddler's melody quickened in pace, the notes spinning and tumbling.

The other three bandits had spaced themselves evenly across the road, barring his horse's path. Jonas slowed his pace only for the moment required for Bronberry to catch up.

"Punch through!" he shouted, and the guard nodded.

The three ragged men charged forward. Jonas blocked the first slash with his blade but missed the second. Fortunately, it clanged off the chain wrapped around his foot. He heard the fiddler laugh as the bows sang again.

Bronberry cursed as an arrow pierced his left thigh. The third bandit had grabbed his horse's bit and had pulled the

SPELL/SWORD

guard to the side. Jonas spun his horse around and moved to assist.

"Come on. We have to get to those archers," he said, stabbing wildly at the third bandit. The man let go of Bronberry's bridle and retreated a few paces. His two companions closed in as well, keeping the two horsemen surrounded. The bandits slashed out with their blades, giving both Jonas and Bronberry a few surface cuts on their exposed shins and forearms. Bronberry's horse was beginning to buck with fear; Jonas desperately grasped for the reins. He happened to be facing in the general direction of the wagon and saw Rime come into view.

Rime stepped calmly from around the corner of the wagon. She raised her hand, as if to point at the archers.

A wind began to blow, howling through the pine needles. The temperature began to drop, from summer to winter in moments. Jonas could see his breath. A ball of white light appeared around the mage's extended hand. It intensified and began to grow -- ice crystals forming and collecting. A spear of blue ice as thick as a tree trunk and twice as long as the wagon. Rime took careful aim then launched it towards the archers.

It whistled through the air and shattered into the side of the pavilion. Two of the archers screamed as razor-shards of ice bit into them. The massive dinosaur bellowed, its head whipping around to inspect the wound. The ice had flash-cauterized the creature's hide. The red blood that dripped down its side came from the two dying archers, steaming slightly where it met with the arcane ice.

The lone surviving archer stood up, holding his side. The fiddler also stood, seeming no worse for wear. The three bandits on the ground were transfixed, staring at Rime.

"Well, well..." the blind man called. "More to you than we were told, it seems. Very well, want to play rough, then we'll play--"

"Shut up," Rime said.

The white light still hung around her hands, and she slowly closed the left into a fist. The light squeezed through the spaces between her fingers, and her hair began to stand on end. Her face was empty and calm.

The fading ice on the dinosaur's side began to reform and spread. The white light in Rime's fist pulsed, and the frost erupted. Long jagged spears of ice plunged deeply into the beast's hide. The long-necked saurian bellowed with pain and leapt forward into the pines. The orange robed fiddler toppled backwards into the pavilion, his instrument giving a final twang. Trees snapped, an avalanche of noise as the beast rushed forward, mad with pain.

The three bandits broke away as well, following the swath of devastation. Jonas rode over to the first bandit he'd wounded. The man inched away, blood oozing from the deep gash in his face. The squire hopped off the horse, landing awkwardly on one foot as he juggled the length of chain with the other.

"End the bastard, "Bronberry ordered.

Jonas pulled the man up. The bandit's beard was thick with blood, but his eyes were clear and full of terror.

"Run. Don't bother us again." He slapped the bleeding man across the shoulders, and the bearded bandit took off at a stuttering run.

"I said..." Bronberry began furiously, and spurred his horse to follow the man. He closed the distance easily and hacked at the man with his axe. The bandit fell screaming. The blonde guard had to get off his horse to finish him, two rough blows. His face looked sick when he turned back. He grabbed his anger to steady himself and stomped across the blood-spattered roadway.

"Follow orders, prisoner. That's the deal, or I'll execute you myself. Are we clear?" A bit of spittle hung from the guard's lower lip.

Jonas turned away in frustration, just in time to see Rime collapse to the ground. Her eyes had rolled into the back of her head and only the whites were showing.

5

The mage drifted on waves of spell-pain. Her mind rolled over and over like a child tumbling down a briar hill. At last the world steadied and Rime opened her eyes.

It was later in the afternoon, and someone had built a fire. The boy was leaning over the older guard, hand probing the wound where the arrow pierced the leg. The guard hissed and leaned hard against the back of the wagon.

"Ow, ow ow... stop it stop it you bastard," Bronberry said.

Jonas ignored his complaints and took a firm grip on the arrow. With a swift motion, he pushed the arrow forward. Rime could see the wicked point coming out the underside of Bronberry's leg.

After a moment of silence, Bronberry howled.

The squire swiftly snapped the arrow head off, then pulled the shaft back out. He calmly wrapped a length of fabric around the guard's leg and stepped away. The blonde man groaned and slowly began to tie off the length of fabric, sweat pouring down his face.

"Where are we?" Rime forced her voice to sound nonplussed.

"About a mile from where we fought." Jonas tossed the bloody arrow into the fire. "We needed to tend to him and you. You're a wizard, then?"

Rime pulled herself up and realized she was sitting in the driver's seat of the wagon with one of her blankets wrapped around her. Humiliation brought a flush to her cheeks.

"Not precisely," she replied, pushing the blanket off her shoulders.

The squire looked at her and said nothing.

"I thought you were just some noble lady, going on a pleasure jaunt," Bronberry said, face tightening with pain as he did the final knot in his bandage. "What do you need us for, if you're so damned powerful?"

Rime stepped down from the wagon, keeping a grip on the side to steady herself. The polished gears of her mind spun, then locked into place.

She stepped gingerly over to the fire and sat down on the ground.

"Well?" Bronberry demanded.

"Wizards. Learned beings who develop magical aptitudes and prowess through years of study and intellectual effort. Primary form of expression: spells. Concrete and rigidly defined codifications of arcane energy, generally broken down by purpose, function and intensity. Different schools of magic have developed, focusing on various applications and specializations. See also Valeria, the City of Lore," she replied.

Bronberry blinked. Then Jonas blinked. The horses also blinked, though no one noticed.

"I am not a wizard," Rime continued. "If you want to be kind, you can refer to me as a mage, the common term for anyone who employs any sort of magical aptitude or skill. But that would not be absolutely correct. There are other words for what I am that are more apt. *Shar'desh* is the Sarmadi word, *Frigjatk* the Old Dwarven, and *Sioba* the surprisingly succinct and lyrical Yad-Elf term. Madwand, wild mage: these are the more common terms you would be familiar with."

The blonde guard stiffened as her words became simpler. "A... a wild mage? Look, girl..."

"And now you are about to say something most unwise." Her eyes reflected the firelight. "I tell you this as a matter of necessity because we go into danger. I have power, yes, but it has a cost. The cost you have just witnessed. Your job is to protect me when I cannot protect myself."

"How long?" Jonas interrupted. "How long are you out?"

Rime turned her attention to the squire. *A fair question and a smart one.*

"It depends. Longer based on the amount of power I use, the complexity, the level of abstraction, and the length of time I employ it."

"Uhh." Jonas said, confused.

Rime continued, "I've been slowly building up my tolerance so that my periods of recovery shouldn't be more than an hour or so. How long was it this time?"

The squire glanced at the sun. "About an hour and a half. Almost two."

The young girl's mouth tightened.

"Well, I've heard enough. I'm going home," Bronberry announced.

"You will not."

"Look here girl. I didn't sign up to guard a walking murder-storm. If we're caught aiding one of your kind..."

"My kind?" Rime spat. "What do you even know about my kind?"

"Not much, except they're bad news," Bronberry stood up with a groan and gingerly put weight on his wounded leg. He started to limp towards his horse, blowing out air with every other step.

"Come on prisoner, if you want to live," The guard managed.

"Double," Rime said quietly.

The blonde guard stopped moving, but did not turn around. He was silent for a few long moments. Then he held out his hand and extended three fingers.

The three travelers pushed on, wanting to put distance between themselves and their fight with the bandits. Though the lost time kept them from reaching the carefully drawn campsite on Rime's mental map, so she settled for a rough "X" when they pulled off the road.

Bronberry proved useful. He backtracked a half-mile from the point they pulled off, ordering Jonas to help him. He showed the squire the trick of cutting a young sapling and using it as a rough broom to scrub the worst of the wagon tracks away.

The two returned to find Rime entering the wagon and locking the door behind her. Jonas immediately set to unhitching the horses as well as seeing to their feed and water from the barrel on the back of the wagon.

The blond guard didn't bother to build another fire, simply digging in his pack for some food and flopped open his bedroll. He unceremoniously chained Jonas to the back of the wagon, manacle around the squire's foot.

"Keep watch," Bronberry grunted, and flopped down.

Bronberry dragged his bedroll well across the clearing, and placed his iron axe within easy reach. Jonas sighed, wondering what special god had made the blonde man. Just enough intelligence to be dangerous, slathered over with horse gut and dog shit. Did the Nameless put such men in the world to test the faithful or simply to amuse itself? The squire couldn't remember any of the pastor's sermons that covered the topic.

The squire sat, leaning against the wagon. He pulled his good steel free from its scabbard and set to honing the edge. The quiet rasp of the whetstone was a comfort.

A few hours passed, and the squire thought of little.

At last the edge of his sword was perfect, and Jonas looked up. The three moons hung over the squire's head. The White Moon was full, Jonas held a thumb up to cover it. Just to the left, the Red Moon was a narrow crescent; the Black Moon was dark, almost invisible above its two brothers. He moved his thumb from moon to moon, blotting each in turn.

Bored, the squire twisted his rump against the earth for the hundredth time. The moth-eaten traveler's cloak smelled terrible. He pulled up the hem of the cloak again and tried to read the name stitched carefully into the lining, but the moonlight was little help. Bronberry had tossed it at him as they'd left the jail. It stank of wet hay, but was warm enough, with a nice deep hood.

Jonas yawned.

He considered trying to wake Bronberry, but he assumed that would end poorly. The guard's loud snores sawed and choked across the clearing. It was about three hours until dawn and long since his watch should have been relieved.

If his throat-saw hasn't attracted any attention, it's probably safe to snatch some sleep now.

Jonas punched his right leg. Three times. An old habit from long watches on the Academy walls. He would keep himself awake. Something to guard, it gave him a feeling of purpose. He would keep the watch, just as he had dug the ditch in Talbot. A simple machine with a simple task.

Rime stared at the ceiling of the wagon.

She had slept in fits and starts, falling from sweaty doze to fragment-dreams. The pieces still floated above her head, drifting and erupting. Little colonies of malformed thoughts vied for control of the wagon's skies.

A wooden bowl full of angry, red-eyed beetles. They clutched chicken bones in their black pincers and waved them angrily at any other nightmares that approached.

A jagged beast, made of forks and knives sharpening itself as it lumbered and slid.

An amorphous pile of green and yellow bile, flies buzzing.

And the hand. The white hand. And the bamboo rod.

Rime pulled the thick blanket up to her chin. She summoned a stream of numbers into the air, and constrained and crushed each vision with bristling computation. The fluorescent green numbers seemed eager to go to battle, their edges crisp and comforting. A web of formulae banished the nightmares, and she closed her eyes. She was guarded by their order. A helpful numeral marched down and daubed the sweat from her brow.

The numbers could protect her from the nightmares at least.

The day grew hot as they traveled. Jonas' mount was

SPELL/SWORD

tethered to the back of the wagon again, and Bronberry rode a few paces ahead. The blonde man was silent, slumped over in the saddle.

Jonas craned his neck around the wagon.

"Where are we going?" he called.

Only silence came from the front of the wagon.

"Hey, you. Rime. I'm not from this country... where are we going?"

He didn't hear her sigh, but it seemed to coalesce in the air and peek over the top of the wagon at him. The sigh shook its head and rolled its vaporous eyes.

"Seriously," he added. "Dangers we could face, lay of the land, anything?"

The wild mage's clipped voice cut cleanly through the air.

"Drift Canyon. Granite and limestone, primary composition. Abandoned quarry and mines, relic of dwarven colony 985 AV. Destroyed by the armies of Carroway as a response to the Sack of Grableton in the Second Mountain Offensive by the Stone Knights of Sypria. Scattered reports of monstrous humanoids, unconfirmed. Length: 24.5 miles."

"And you need to get to the other side?"

"Yes."

"And we can't go around?"

"No time."

53

"Time? What's the hurry?"

No sound but the grind of the wagon wheels. Jonas leaned as far as possible out of the saddle, trying to see up to the driver's seat.

"What's the hurry?" he repeated.

The imagined sigh loomed larger, and Jonas could picture its murderous look, icicles dripping off its nose. It shook its head once, twice. The squire settled back into his saddle.

The stone of the canyons was a deep, midnight blue shot through with veins of humble granite. It rose from the surrounding evergreens like a child's sand castle, tumbledown and irregular. Rime calmly explained the geological history of these canyons. The entire range of stone had been extruded from the earth, pushed up by the subterranean travels of the Mongar, a race of giant sized moles.

"Wait,wait, wait... moles?" Bronberry demanded. "Fucking moles?"

"Giant moles, yes," Rime said. "The historical text was quite clear."

Jonas scratched the prickly stubble on his face and concealed a grin. Then, realizing he was behind the wagon and completely out of view, grinned even wider.

SPELL/SWORD

The squire looked over the top of the wagon, where he could make out the upper reaches of the canyon walls. He quickly spotted several dilapidated structures. A tin shack gutted by rust, overflowing with a purple creeper vine. Half a rope bridge, wooden slats hanging down in a grand leer. The stone of the canyons was clearly different from all the surrounding lands. Dark blue stone, and here and there amongst the granite were smoke-green crystals. Jonas brought his horse alongside the front of the wagon, as the guard and mage continued to discuss matters of geographic import.

"I don't care if the book said the giant moles had massive banjos playing 'Red Tiger and the Lady' while cooking muffins on a ceramic oven shaped like Seto's tits. That is the dumbest thing that I have ever heard." Bronberry crossed his arms with finality.

"This conversation is a waste of time," Rime said. "That blind bandit won't be the last. There are sure to be others hunting me."

She climbed back into the driver's seat and flicked the reins. Jonas shook his head.

"Just giant moles -- or are there voles as well? How about groundhogs? Diggerpigs? Giant diggerpigs?" The guard chomped down on his jerky and snorted.

The three travellers entered the Drift Canyons.

Ten minutes later it started to rain.

THE ASSASSIN OF TIME WELL SPENT

The grand airship hung above a city filled with smoke, steel, and brick. It was a dreadnought; a massive ship designed for assault and intimidation, not for speed. A gigantic green skull was painted on both sides of the hull, and the twenty cannons barrels poking out of their slots were enameled a similar hue.

On deck, the Green Skulls stood at attention. They were a well disciplined crew, clean rows and cleaner brass buttons gleaming on their verdant coats. Teeth were clenched, eyes thick with anger -- but still their discipline held as they watched the execution. Their captain had been murdered, not more than twenty minutes before, and they would honor her training even as they relished the punishment being meted out on the assassin by their first mate.

A broad plank had been run out from the deck, and the killer was bound and knelt on the end. Below the city of Quorum and the wide bay of dirty water. The first mate, a minotaur, nearly tore the shoulder out of his aeronaut coat with the force with which he raised the sword high above the assassin's head.

SPELL/SWORD

The assassin was dressed in purposefully innocuous gray leathers, supple and well-oiled. Thick enough to slow a blade, but light as a shadow. The minotaur had ripped off the hood before raising the sword, revealing a face that was painfully noticeable: burnt orange skin, and red eyes the color of ketchup. Two bony protrusions mushroomed from his brow; a bard would call them devil's horns, but they looked more like sea coral, misshapen and twisted. They were a pain whenever he needed to conceal his profile, but they had turned more than a few killing blows and Sideways was quite proud of them. He often painted them a garish blue, though he had opted for a muted brown for this particular assignment.

"Any last words?" the black-furred minotaur demanded. "You miserable devil-spawned life-taker?"

"Is that sword clean?" the assassin asked.

"You...!" the minotaur bellowed and brought the sword down with all his might.

Sideways caught the sword blade between his teeth and turned his head sharply to the left. It snapped clean, leaving the hilt and a ragged foot of steel in his attacker's hand. The broken blade spun easily in his mouth, sticking out like a metal tongue. He gripped it firmly and whipped his head forward like a psychotic ostrich.

The blade punched firmly into the thick black hair of the minotaur's hide. Sideways gritted his teeth and started to twist, but a thick blow to the back of his head forced him to spit out the broken sword blade or risk an immediate lobotomy. A few gouges inside his mouth began to bleed, small payment.

The assassin stood up, taking advantage of the brief

57

respite. The angry minotaur smelled faintly of nutmeg, pawing roughly at the shallow wound in its thigh. Sideways watched the broken hilt clatter on the steel deck, a ragged tooth. A few of the younger cadets wore surprised expressions at the unexpected interruption. The older Skulls were stone-faced, waiting patiently for their First Mate to finish the job.

Sideways smiled, his teeth a cheerful, bloody ruin. It did a lot to improve his mood, if not his appearance.

"Moo," he said.

Minotaurs hate it when you say 'moo'.

"Moooooooo." Sideways waggled his horns at the first mate.

The first mate's horns were much more attractive than the devil-kin's. He was treated to a closer look as the minotaur bellowed with rage and charged, head lowered, massive black-haired arms held wide to grab and crush.

The orange-skin assassin kicked off into a dead run, closing the distance. He tucked his head forward and somersaulted over the wide back of the first mate. The minotaur tried to stop, pickle-green hooves skidding on the studded metal plank, stopping inches from the open air. Sideways flipped the broken sword hilt up with his toe, kicking it a couple of feet in the air. He spun, and kicked the hilt again, directly into the flailing backside of the minotaur.

The first mate roared with pain and instinctively jumped forward -- off the end of the plank.

SPELL/SWORD

The assassin turned to face the forty Green Skulls and bent forward so they could see his bound hands.

"Any of you air-dogs believe in sportsmanship?" he asked.

Kitchen-sink clatter as metal blades came out of sheaths. Sideways scratched his chin pensively on his breastbone.

"Guess not." The assassin spared a thought for the black minotaur falling toward the city below. Wouldn't it be grand if he landed in some fancy Yad-Elf's tea party, or on some pastor's sermon? A world of stories with ends that he would never know.

The best strategy for fighting two score trained warriors is to employ an explosive device, preferably delivered by cannon while one sips chilled fruit juice from safe distance and glances through a spy-glass. A servant with hot towels and a basket of treats is also recommended. The second best strategy also employs ranged tactics -- a unit of trained archers, three or four slaughter-wizards, even a regiment of trained riflemen if you have the coin. The third best strategy is to have four score warriors on your side, higher terrain and a dedicated cavalry comprised of acid-breathing geckos. When the tides of battle remove these strategies as viable options, a seasoned general adapts. Or adopts the fourth best strategy, a total retreat followed by contacting a scribe-house with a rough draft of your war memoir.

Okay, got my hands tied. Problem one. They took my swords, need to get those. Problem two. Lots of pointy metal coming my way. Problem three. Problem four--

Blades cut through the air, but Sideways wasn't there anymore.

His shoulders bent oddly, limbs sliding at strange angles as he half rolled, half slid across the deck -- leaping up like a fish, then bending and turning around the warriors, around the steel. The Green Skulls collided with each other, feet tangling as they tried to catch the gray leather.

Sideways spun, his hip on the deck, and kicked the back of a nearby aeronaut's knees. The woman crumpled in pain, and her cutlass clattered to the deck. The devil-kin continued his momentum and scooped up the weapon ably with his bound hands. The rope parted with a snap.

The stolen cutlass whirled in his orange hands, and the Skulls pulled back in alarm, leaving a clear space around the assassin. The blank metal spun, blurring the green uniforms in his vision.

Sideways felt an overpowering urge to say something cool. But battlefield bravado is best saved for the stage. Killers save their breath.

The cutlass blurred as he lunged, and a throat opened. He spun, and an arm was ruined. Two faces were split and hewn. Blood and green uniforms began to litter the deck. A red-haired dwarf managed to parry his blade, earning a shattered clavicle and a long gash across his white belly as reward.

The assassin would have preferred to avoid the carnage. A hang glider had brought him right up the belly of the dreadnought airship. The assassin had slid through an exhaust pipe, and silent as a shadow into the stateroom of his quarry. A quick thrust with a poniard, and the fat old woman had burbled her last.

But then, the dog. And the barking.

A severed hand flopped on the assassin's shoulder. It

SPELL/SWORD

wasn't his so he ignored it. He was far more concerned about the state of his borrowed cutlass. The previous owner had kept it reasonably well, sharp enough for sharp work on a boarding party, or across a merchant's throat, but the simple steel was beginning to chip and buckle. The frenzied slash and parry of his endless circle was eating away at the poor weapon. Sideways estimated that he'd killed or incapacitated eight or nine of the Skull warriors, but a brace of garden-green uniforms pushed and stamped, seeking to overpower him. Time to even the odds, time to retrieve his proper tools.

The devil-kin flung the chipped cutlass at the crowd's feet, hoping to nick a few ankles and buy himself precious seconds. Without pausing, he leaped through the glass porthole directly behind him. He had been studiously maneuvering himself closer and closer to it for the past several maimings. The glass circle seemed barely wide enough for a large cat to squeeze through, but the devilkin's joints bent and broke to form himself into a slender arrow of force, rocketing through.

He was in a narrow hallway, the same he had been dragged and kicked down after the barking dog incident. They had ripped his swords from the rope bag on his back and tossed them in a locker until after the execution.

That locker. The one with the white crease down the center where some heavy object had fallen against it. Another story -- one with a beginning he would never know.

But he knew how this story ended. He headbutted the locker door. It buckled and gave up a hand hold. Clever fingers slipped in and pulled. The metal whined in protest, and he peered in to see the hilts of his two swords.

61

"A lot of help you were -- time to go to work, lazy swords." He grunted, peeling the locker door back another handspan. *Problem two - solved.* Farther down the hall, a door burst open and a dozen Skulls lumbered in, swords held cautiously, knuckles white. *Right, problem three.*

Sideways grabbed both swords with one hand; the hilts were narrow. He pulled them free and let the bent locker door flap back into place.

Both blades were short, suitable for close quarters work. One ignited in red flame as the devil-kin hissed its name. *"Sunhammer."*

The other sword was named Chester, Chet for short, and needed no instruction. It was gray on the edges and gray in the center.

The assassin trotted down the hall, and allowed himself a short line of dialogue, simply because it would hopefully further distract his opponents and keep them off-balance.

"Excuse me, which way is the lavatory?"

Classic Sideways, the assassin thought as Sunhammer neatly sheared through four of the sky pirates' cutlasses. The first Skulls screamed in pain as the flaming blade's heat flash-fried their hands and any exposed flesh. One dark-skinned Skull was blinded instantly, eyes boiling in their sockets.

Sideways crinkled his nose in disgust. *Well, at least he won't see Chet go to work.*

The gray blade sang through the air with a stone's glee.

SPELL/SWORD

The dreadnought, *Avalanche*, moved drunkenly towards the port. The vast Mohinder Bay, surrounded on both arms by the grimy buildings of the city. Sideways was an excellent assassin, but a terrible pilot. The airship listed heavily to the right, and several green uniformed corpses tumbled across the deck and over the side.

"Shit!" The devil-kin spun the giant wheel in the other direction trying to correct the ship's course.

Bodies tumbled over each other towards the opposite rail, like bloody sacks of flour. The dreadnought was heading directly for a water tower on the edge of the city.

The assassin couldn't think of any strategies for coping with an oncoming water tower. His gray form dove off the deck into the dirty waters of the bay.

The airship collided with the water tower in a cataclysmic scream of metal. The great dome of the tower toppled forward, slamming into the bay like a giant drum. The dreadnought slowly spun around the tower's base, fire and smoke pouring out of its wounded underbelly. Sideways poked his head back out of the water just in time to see the main engines of the *Avalanche* explode, vast oily columns of super-heated fuel illuminating the waterfront. The assassin applauded.

Then he noticed the dirty water of the bay beginning to ignite, and he swam quickly for the shoreline.

Waiting for him were a dozen drunken sailors and five constables from the Copper Garrison. The devil-kin recognized them from the brightly polished copper halfhelms they wore. They were all Yad-Elves, children of

63

the forest, or would be if they didn't live here in the smokestack studded city of Quorum. Sideways sighed and reached over his shoulder for Sunhammer and Chet.

"Constables. I advise you to not engage this foe." A clean voice, even and perfectly audible. A voice that wasn't raised often. A familiar voice. A deadly voice.

Linus stepped past the gathered sailors and stood between the assassin and the constables. He wore flat gray armor and no helm on his head. The thin gray hair on his head was matted and damp. A constable stepped forward but instantly recoiled when the old man held out something in his hand. She pushed back her copper helm and signalled for her men to fall back. The gray knight tucked away his badge of office. Sideways tried not to roll his eyes. *First time you've seen one of those, eh wood elf? Quite some time since anyone has.*

Linus turned to the assassin.

"You're hired."

"Yeah," Sideways sighed. "Guess I am."

6

"This is a wonderful day. Really! I am having a delightful time." Bronberry yelled to be heard over the pounding rain.

"Stay focused," Rime said. "You, in the back... keep your eyes on the sides of the canyon."

The sun was setting, but to their surprise, the green crystals in the granite emitted a chilly, lime-colored light, enough to make out the immediate surroundings of the trail, but not to provide any comforting visibility to the many open mine shafts that gaped in the canyon walls.

Rime bit her tongue and did not respond further to the guard's sarcasm. A tiny awning over the driver's seat kept the worst of the rain off, but her boots were getting soaked. The limelight crystals were an unexpected boon, and she was determined to take advantage of the time they could save.

The mage turned suddenly towards the right side of the canyon. Something had moved. Her eye caught it, even though her mind was distracted. Rime considered not mentioning it; it was sure to make the obnoxious guard feel vindicated.

Her eyes scanned the canyon wall and hovered over a narrow stone shelf connecting two dark tunnel openings. Two bushes grew into a tangled mass in between, blocking the green crystalline light. The rain made the leaves move like writhing worms.

The green leaves exploded as a dark figure shot across the stone shelf. Rime caught a flash of bulbous skin and the shine of metal on its head, back, and feet. It moved with great speed, and a faint whirring sound tickled their ears.

Jonas appeared at the right of the driver's seat, his sword out.

"Get ready," he said as he grabbed the team's bridles, pulling them to the side of the canyon.

The sound of whirring, metal on stone, like a wind-up toy across the polished marble of her father's ballroom.

A figure appeared on the left side of the canyon, leaning over another shelf a dozen feet above their heads. A long spear, made of brass and covered with odd components was first, followed by the pulpy face of a hideous frog. The creature was wearing a crude brass helmet, studded with bolts, and bulky gauntlets grasped the spear. Rime spotted a tube running from the butt of the spear into the bottom of a massive rectangular device strapped to its back.

"It's a refrigerator!" Bronberry said.

"It's *not* a refrigerator," Rime hissed.

SPELL/SWORD

A jet of steam screamed from the right side of the frog's backpack, and it flung itself down towards the canyon floor.

It was wearing roller skates.

Giant boots, studded with brass, with cunning steel wheels that dug into the walls of the canyon. The frog skated right down the side, croaking a challenge.

Bronberry took a moment and turned to the young mage.

"I hate you," he said.

Jonas moved to intercept as the guard pulled his axe free of its harness. The frog's spear ignited with fierce yellow electricity. As Jonas approached, the creature screamed, lowered the point of the spear and put on more speed.

Sword clanked against spear, and Jonas spun, trying to dodge. The electric blade punched into his left shoulder, tearing a deep gash. The squire dropped to the ground, knees thudding against the canyon floor.

The frog creature croaked excitedly, made a sharp turn and came to a complete stop facing the wounded squire. A spray of stones and mud spattered against the wagon.

Bronberry spurred his horse forward and swung down with his axe, but missed completely. The frog kicked off, a cloud of steam propelling it forward. Jonas wheeled himself around, blood dripping from his left arm. He switched to a two-handed grip on his sword and braced himself.

Rime stepped down from the wagon and took careful aim. Firmly supporting her left hand with her right, she extended one finger. Her brow furrowed with concentration. *Just a small drop.*

A single ray of red energy shot from her finger, no wider than a thimble.

It hit the frog's backpack, and the brass and steel exploded. A violent cloud of steam burst forth, throwing the frog to the ground. The yellow electricity dissipated, and the frog lay there stunned.

Jonas moved swiftly, and placed his sword at the base of the creature's neck, right below the elaborate bronze helmet.

"Do you yield?" he said.

"Graaaaak!" the frog replied weakly.

"Boy. We don't have time. This thing's friends are coming! Kill it, and then we run," Bronberry said furiously.

Rime exhaled and leaned slightly against the wagon.

"Yes, quickly," she said.

Jonas looked up in surprise.

"But he's unarmed. He yielded to me. I can't kill him now. It would... it would be wrong."

The sound of rain and the roar of more steam-powered skates filled the pause.

Rime pointed a finger at the frog. A red burst.

"I can. Now ride. We have to make it through this canyon

SPELL/SWORD

before they catch us."

Bronberry spurred his horse forward as the mage weakly pulled herself up into the driver's seat. Jonas stared at the dead frog in mute shock.

The limelight refracted through the rain and made the canyon a green nightmare. Ahead stuttering shadows danced against the midnight canyon walls.

Jonas clung to his horse and tried to keep track of their pursuers. The roar of their steam-powered skates, the occasional crackle of their lightning spears jutting over an escarpment, or darting down into the open mouth of a tunnel. The frogs were close.

The canyon bent sharply to the right, and Rime snapped the reins to encourage the team to move swiftly through the turn. Bronberry's horse screamed as the guard pulled up and cursed. The wagon pulled to the left and stopped, horses bellowing.

A throng of the frogs waited, grinding back and forth in place as if to keep their wheels loose. Several spear-frogs nearly flew across the rocky floor of the canyon, moving in wide circles -- first large, then small. A few larger frogs hovered closest to a massive chunk of the green crystal that lit the area with verdant intensity. Splayed on top of the crystal was a massive toad, easily five times larger than any of the others. It wore a pair of ornate brass gauntlets, anvil-sized fingers tapping idly on the side of its crystal throne.

"That's a big toad," Jonas said, pulling his horse up close

to the wagon.

Rime and Bronberry shot him synchronized looks of murderous disdain.

"GRAAAACK," the massive creature opened its jaws, revealing a slimy interior that slid back into utter darkness. A million miles of night in the back of the frog's throat.

The smaller frogs gyrated and spun in some ritual of fealty or worship. A few on the nearest periphery had caught sight of the three travelers and seemed to be waiting on the proper caesura in their amphibian round to skate forward and attack.

"Our only chance is to break through to the other side. The canyon seems to narrow past this point, and we can better defend ourselves in a bottleneck," Rime said. "You two in front. Don't let them stop the wagon."

Jonas nodded. Bronberry wiped rainwater out of his face and managed a sickly grin.

"Easy enough, right?" the guard replied.

The two men on horseback kicked their mounts into a canter, and Rime snapped the wagon reins sharply.

The massive throng of frogs reacted sluggishly to their assault. The outer line of skaters halted their ritual movements immediately, but left large gaps in between spear-frogs. Jonas felt a brief surge of elation. If they kept their speed up, they might be able to pass through unscathed.

That was when Bronberry wheeled his horse around and kicked off savagely back in the direction they had come.

No time to react; they were only a few dozen yards from the first of the frogs. The squire pulled his horse directly in front of the wagon team, and held his sword ready. Jonas tried to ignore the pain in his shoulder.

Two frogs came in on his right, steel wheels singing. He tried to strike at them with his sword, but they pulled out of reach. The two caught themselves against the front corner of the wagon and spun off into the mud, lightning spears jangling and sparking. The wagon rocked slightly from the impact. Rime clutched the side of the driver's seat until the wagon resettled on all four wheels. Jonas whipped his head back around in time to parry an incoming spear from the left. Somehow the crackling energy of the spear had a smell, a burnt smell, like day-old coffee.

Jonas grimaced as the spear continued its movement, ripping through the hem of his cloak and scoring a long gouge on his horse's flank. The roan screamed in pain and jumped hard to the right. The squire gripped the pommel of his saddle, and tried not to fall off. The wagon pulled past him, while he wrestled with the wounded mare.

The gigantic toad bellowed again, bringing the mad ritual to a halt. It banged its gauntlets together and pointed in the direction of the fleeing wagon. With mad fervor, the steam-armored frogs lunged forward, wheels digging into the hard granite of the canyon floor.

Jonas regained control of his wounded mount and saw that the throng of frogs were only a few spans behind him. The squire slammed his heels into the roan's sides, forcing her into a gallop.

The throaty cries of the frog-men were in his ears. He

spotted a brace of them skating on the canyon wall, brass spears dragging a trail behind them. They would converge on the wagon within moments.

The roan's desperate speed closed the gap, and Jonas saw Rime sitting quite calmly in the driver's seat. The reins dangled loosely in her right hand.

A nimbus of green energy was coalescing around her head, reminding him of thorns. The mage stared straight ahead, seeing nothing.

"Rime! This is not a good idea! Rime! Rime!" he yelled, trying to ignore the roar of the steam-skates.

The wagon was only a few score feet from the canyon's bottleneck. The frogs descended, skidding along the canyon wall; clouds of steam propelling them forward. Jonas saw Rime lift her hand as if in slow motion and snap her fingers.

From the muddy earth, from the canyon walls, from all around the wagon dozens of earthen hands stretched forth, grasping and clawing. The wave of brass-armored frogs broke on the hands, green bubble-faces popping with cries of pain and surprise. Jonas watched as a frog nearing the wagon was plucked into the air by two stone hands and pulled apart. Slimy innards fell amid an explosion of steam as the back canister ruptured. The squire felt his stomach turn as his roan thundered between the hands and amphibian detritus fell around him. A few of the frogs managed to evade the hands and continued the pursuit, but the bulk of the attackers were stopped.

Jonas looked left to congratulate the young mage. Her slim form was bent forward, completely unconscious. The wagon reins fell from her nerveless white hands as they bounced on the edge of the seat.

The squire looked forward. The bottleneck was only a few yards away. He made a quick choice and sheathed his sword.

With a feeling of regret, Jonas jumped across to the driver's seat. The roan bolted wide to the right and was impaled by the lead frogs' spears. *Poor lady. Didn't even name her.*

Rime flopped to one side. The squire had to move quickly to keep her from flying off the wagon. She felt like she was made of cloth and air. A few hurried breaths and he managed to grab the reins. Jonas pulled sharply to the right to avoid the edge of the bottleneck. The team made it just in time, but the back end of the wagon collided with the stone wall and teetered dangerously on two wheels.

The squire snapped the reins hard, and the two horses' speed pulled the wagon back to earth.

The sides of the canyon were close. Chunks of green crystal stuck out and shattered against the wooden sides of the wagon. Jonas tried to peer ahead through the rain.

Then he heard it.

The roar of steam-skates, a dozen feet above, moving along the top rim of the canyon.

I have no idea how long this canyon is, or if we're anywhere close to the exit. These frogs know the terrain and aren't having any trouble keeping up with us. Gotta change the board.

The crystal limelight shone down the stony aisle of the canyon, and the squire spotted the opening to a tunnel. It was small. If he was on horseback he would need to duck to go inside. It looked only slightly smaller than the wagon itself.

Jonas stared at the tunnel mouth. He looked over at Rime's unconscious form and stared at the tunnel again.

The squire snapped the reins, hoping the exhausted horses wouldn't panic.

He Who Croaks in Darkness lumbered along the canyon floor, led by the small-ones. His gauntlets dragged through the mud, as he hopped with profound dignity. The small-ones jabbered at him, pointing at the problem with their shock-spears.

The little wooden box with wheels was broken, and jammed into a tunnel-mouth. A few small-ones were hacking at the wood with their spears, but it would take them some time to bash their way into the tunnel.

He Who Croaks in Darkness thought. Hard. Nearby frogs began to grab their helmets in pain. The headgear had been designed to allow the tribe to operate within His proximity, but when the master toad concentrated, it quickly wore through their defenses.

"Graaaak." He decided, and the small-ones obeyed.

They stopped digging at the tunnel's plug and moved further down the canyon.

He Who Croaks in Darkness had spoken.

7

The horses died.

The first had tumbled into a crevasse and had been hung by its own tackle. The second had broken its two front legs and filled the cavern with hideous screaming. Jonas had pulled himself forward in a daze and gave the poor beast mercy. The squire turned away from the dying horse and sheathed his sword. Absently he clutched at his left hand. Two fingers were bent at a painful angle.

Luckily his legs were unharmed, and a few green crystals provided enough illumination to see the shattered rubble of the wagon wedged inside the tunnel entrance. The wooden frame, trapped in the opening, had brought down a fair amount of stone and earth to fill the other spaces. The frog-men would not be following, so that part of his plan had worked at least. He moved towards the wagon and tripped over Rime.

The young mage was laying face down on the ground. Jonas rolled her over, and saw that her delicate face had been roughly scratched and bruised by the tunnel floor. He checked her arms and legs, but she seemed to have sustained no other damage from being flung off the wagon.

Her eyes opened slowly, the pupils rapidly dilated. She grabbed a fistful of the squire's shirt.

"Water. Get it. Now."

Jonas smiled in relief, and pulled her up to a sitting position. He leaned her against a waist-high crystal and went to poke around the shattered wagon for supplies.

"How long?" she asked.

"Really short this time. Maybe twenty minutes?" The squire moved towards the wagon.

"Good. That's good. Why is the wagon... where are... the frogs..." Rime closed her eyes.

Jonas returned with one of the girl's blankets bundled into an impromptu haversack. He placed a skin of water into the mage's hands and carefully shook Rime back awake.

"Don't drink too much., I could only find the one. A couple of broken loaves, a half a wheel of yellow cheese, a belt knife, this blanket -- and this." He held his hand forth, showing a few gold coins.

Rime took a short pull from the waterskin and narrowed her eyes.

"All lost in the crash," she said.

"I guess Bronberry made the smart play." He tucked the coins into the blanket-sack and held his hand down to the weary girl.

Rime ignored his hand and pushed herself up the crystal outcropping. "I'll deal with that one later. Give me the knife."

Jonas looked down the tunnel. A narrow stone bridge spanned a dark chasm, leading to a ragged opening that showed almost no green light.

"You destroyed my wagon," Rime said flatly, tucking the small dagger in her belt. "I loved that wagon."

"I didn't have much choice..." Jonas began.

"I'm sure there was a better option, but you just couldn't see it through your sheep-dog hair. Now we're trapped in this tunnel and have no idea how to get out."

"Path goes that way. Hopefully, it'll connect up with some other mining tunnels, and we'll find our way out." Jonas replied. *I saved your life, girl.*

"Hope. Wonderful. Hope is your plan." The mage moved to the wagon rubble and pried forth a pair of slim boards, thin enough to hold comfortably.

She grabbed chunks of the green crystal and wedged it forcefully into the end of each board. Rime tossed one of the impromptu torches to Jonas and set her shoulders.

"How can I trust you? You know that I have no money now, and your freedom waits as soon as we find the exit." Her face was resolute in the green light.

Jonas pulled his hood out from underneath his collar. At some point in the night's excitement, it had gotten pushed down. He shrugged at Rime.

"I don't know. We're still in danger now, and it'll be better if we work together."

"But when we escape, what then? I still have a long way to go."

"I said I'd go with you," Jonas said with surprise. "I made a promise."

A dull thud sounded from the mouth of the tunnel. The sound was followed by the sharp noises of spears digging into the sides of the tunnel and the rear of the shattered wagon outside. Jonas took a few steps towards the sound, waiting to see if any of the frogs could pry their way in. Rime's expression was unreadable when he turned back.

"My only good fortune is that you are an idiot." The mage moved towards the ragged opening, and he followed.

Rime and Jonas set out together, across the stone bridge into the darkness.

***

Bronberry rode through the rain.

He did not look back, and he only stopped when his horse was too exhausted to run any further.

The next morning the rain stopped, and he kept going.

The mage and squire made their slow way down the mine shaft. Green light from their torches revealed little of any interest, other than the occasional wooden timber bracing the roof and the clear sign of hammer and pick on the stone walls. A section had partially collapsed, forcing the two to clamber over a pile of stones on their stomachs. Jonas turned to pull Rime across the last few feet, but then thought better of it. The girl pulled herself across and panted for a moment on her hands and knees.

Jonas checked the binding on his shoulder while she caught her breath. The wound was ugly but not deep. He made a note to wash it thoroughly when he found enough clean water -- the field surgeon's voice hammered into him still: *A dirty wound is a dead soldier, cadet.* He prayed that his fingers weren't broken.

Rime stood and moved past Jonas. He tucked the edges of his bandage back and followed. The shaft continued, angling downward.

The mage stopped and inspected a wooden cross-beam. Thick runes had been carved into the wood. Jonas leaned his torch close to increase the light. Rime nodded once and continued down the tunnel.

The squire stared at the runes a moment.

"So... can you read these?" he called.

"Yes."

"What do they say?"

"*Draedun. Kort mind-far. Bek.*"

Boot-leather sounded on stone as the squire trotted to catch up with Rime. He looked at her, then at the walls, then at his feet. A few more paces, and he cleared his throat.

"Ahh... what does that..."

He realized that the mage was behind him, nose inches from the tunnel floor, digging at the base of a stone with her hands. She pried forth a small lump, and held it up to her torch. She looked pleased.

"What's that?" he asked. "More rock?"

"It's *draedun*. Olistone in the common tongue." Rime stood up, still holding the stone.

The stone was brown. Supremely brown.

"I don't know what..." Jonas attempted.

Rime continued down the tunnel.

The squire barked a laugh, and ran a hand across his face. A kernel of irritation warmed his stomach. The mage reminded him of several instructors and scholars at the academy. Quickly tiring of the curly-haired youth's plodding mind, they tended to ignore or dismiss his questions out of hand. When Jonas had stubbornly persisted, the laughter of the other recruits burned. He hated not understanding and he hated the flush on his face. Jonas felt like he was building a bridge across a river. The planks were heavy and easily slipped from his hand, but he would grimly push himself into the icy water to pick them back up and slam them in place. Only when the bridge was complete would he cross the river. The only faint compliment he had ever received was from Scholar

80

Dryden. The gaunt old Yad-Elf had laid a hand on his shoulder and said, "At least when you finally learn something, you learn it all the way."

Jonas plunged into that river again and caught up with the slim girl.

"What is Olistone? And why is it important?"

"It's used in forge-work. 43.2 on the Werntz-Plassco hardness scale. It conducts almost no heat, so it's perfect for building stoves, smelting devices, and molt-conduits. It's why the dwarves built the mine here. It is only found in conjunction with granite bathyspheres. Likelihood of crystal formation practically zero." Rime recited.

"Uh. Yeah. So it's like pitchstone?"

The mage looked piercingly at the squire.

"What is pitchstone?"

"My dad used it when he built the new fireplace. He said it would keep the fire from burning through the walls. I dropped a piece, and he gave me a good smack on the side of my head." Jonas grinned.

The mage's eyes went blank as she absorbed this information. Her mind ran its fingers down the long, long row of books and pulled out the volume in question. A silver quill made a notation in the margins of the pertinent entry. *Possible colloquial variant name: Pitchstone. Source unreliable.*

"But why are you making such a big deal about it?" Jonas continued, kicking a stray stone across the tunnel floor. "It's expensive, but you can get it in just about any general store."

Very unreliable, the quill added.

"Because it means the verdant crystals we've encountered didn't occur naturally. There's no way they would form in this kind of stone. It's as likely as finding a polar bear in the Sarmadi sands." Rime trailed off as she saw the squire's blank stare. "Big glowy green rocks. Not supposed to be here. Get it?"

The kernel of irritation grew a little larger. Jonas clenched his fist.

"So?" he said.

"So? What do you mean 'so'? It's a startling discovery-- "

"That doesn't seem to be useful right now?" Jonas finished.

"All information is useful. It weighs nothing and fits everywhere. Wait." The mage stopped and pointed down the mine shaft. "I feel a draft. Probably a larger chamber. Hold my torch."

Jonas took the torch and watched as Rime crept forward.

He felt another plank slip from his hands into the water.

Rime blinked rapidly, forcing her pupils to dilate. As the steady green light of the torches faded behind, she began to see the the outlines of a square stone portal leading into the next chamber. She ran her hands over the stone and felt several deeply carved runes. They were dwarven, but

SPELL/SWORD

her tired fingers couldn't make them out. She leaned against the right side of the portal and craned her head slowly around to peer into the chamber.

The light seemed to be coming primarily from a waterfall on the far side of the chamber. Large clumps of yellow fungus adorned the cave wall around and behind the waterfall, each giving off a dim yellow light. A small pool filled one end of the cavern. *The tributary to a subterranean river. Possible escape route.* Rime's turned her attention to the rest of the chamber.

A simple staircase made from wooden beams led from the portal to the floor of the chamber. Three exits: two square doorways like the mage's perch, and the third was a fresh mine shaft. In the center of the chamber was a small wooden building. Nearby was a fire pit, surrounded by simple wooden stools.

She slipped quietly around the stone door frame. The sound of falling water was all she heard. A thin veneer of dust and debris covered the shack, stools, and floor. In the fungal light she easily spotted a few fat cavefish swimming in the pool.

Rime looked down at her right hand. It was gripping the edge of the doorway tightly. Her breathing was accelerated. As she considered her vision, a cloudy fog seemed to cover the edges. The next rough-hewn step in front of her seemed to waver. She looked at her left hand, it clenched forcefully. Will made her vision steady.

These cold facts rolled through her mind, and the inevitable assessment emerged.

She was exhausted. It was time to stop.

83

Rime continued down the stairs and moved to the fire pit. She sat on a stool. This place would serve.

A few minutes later, Jonas poked his head into the chamber. He had tucked both crystal torches under his arm, and had drawn his sword. The second torch kept slipping, and he had to stop several times to awkwardly catch it and tuck it back into place.

The girl sat on a stool, her head leaned forward. She was asleep.

THE WIZARD OF LEFT OR RIGHT

The eyes followed the woman down the street. Old man eyes, little boy eyes -- leaning, tilting, corkscrew eyes, the eyes ringed with drink, the eyes of gutter-flame, the eyes, the eyes, the eyes.

They always did. A slimy algae on top of the river. She was accustomed to it.

Cotton stopped to inspect a pair of clay urns, garishly painted with a circle of green elephants. The merchant was brown as a nut, broken smile instant and wide, a tuft of gray hair jutting from his chin. He leaned a little too close, eager to peer at her breasts as she leaned over.

She locked her eyes on his and forced him to look up. The merchant noticed her gaze but still finished a thorough survey.

Cotton's lips kinked. The merchant was old, and his single-minded determination was amusing.

The sun was hot on her back, her short-cropped colorless

85

blonde hair dripped. Gorah was an old city, a baked-clay horror. Desert surrounded the city, and the ocean to the south did little to alleviate the heat. Gorah was a port city. Merchants and travellers from all across the globe gathered and mingled and lied and cheated each other; new marks delivered fresh with each passing tide.

"How much?"

"For such a beautiful lady -- it breaks my heart in a thousand, thousand pieces of offal -- but I fear the best price I can offer is thirty *ptoch*," the merchant sang out, the theatre of the marketplace.

Cotton's lips kinked again. The merchant was a treasure, a sentinel of the old ways. Very well, she would play her part.

"Thirty gold pieces?" she said, horrified. "For these cracked pieces of pottery, stolen from a child's grave in the dead of night by bandits and crudely re-painted by blind simpletons?"

The merchant's dark eyes grew wet, and he looked at her with new-found respect. The old man had to lean on the edge of his cart for a moment and collect himself for a proper response. Cotton waited patiently.

"My... *mother*... painted these urns with her own broken hands, with her dying breath she pushed these into my arms. These urns slosh with the tears I spilled on that saintly woman's death bed!" The merchant covered his eyes, palms outward.

Masterful.

"Was your mother suffering from some sort of palsy? The

SPELL/SWORD

paint is uneven and slopes around the pot like..." Cotton searched for a sufficiently deprecating simile, and felt the back of her neck tingle.

She leapt nimbly over the table, pushing the urn into the surprised arms of the merchant. A metal fist erupted from the ground where she had been standing moments before.

Cotton tossed her purse into the urn. "Deliver this to the Library of Illuminated Lion's Breath, care of Mezzo, the secretary. And take care to leave the purse and my change, after removing twenty *ptoch*."

The metal fist opened, wide as a wagon -- cracked, dry clay falling off the fingers. The metal was powder blue, pock-marked with corrosion and rust. The joints spun, intricate mechanisms dancing.

"Twenty?!?" The merchant began with stoic indifference to the approaching machine.

This merchant was truly a gem. Cotton undid her white cloak, laying it primly on a handy tent pole. "We would've agreed on twelve after the third act. I'm paying an extra three for delivery -- and five more out of respect and admiration for a true businessman."

The nut-brown merchant grinned and bowed before making a quick exit.

The street was in an uproar as the machine pulled itself from the packed earth. It was roughly man-shaped, though much larger. Two squat legs and a filthy glass cockpit for a head. The machine only had one arm. A massive fist of garish blue steel, cracked stone falling from its clenching fingers. A furious drill was mounted to the center of its torso. Traders hurriedly packed up their stalls, children clambering on top of nearby buildings for a better view, one mother screamed for her daughter to come down at once.

Cotton moved her hands through the strange positions required by her craft and spoke the secret words.

Her eyes blazed with yellow light, and she saw her death. In thirty seconds, in two minutes, in five -- the heavy blue fist of the machine pulping her to nothing -- badly painted pottery flying everywhere, tripping over a tent rope and the machine's cruel drill spinning over her. Echoes of the future, possible paths, places she stood where the blue machine would leave her broken and bleeding. They spun out in front of her, gleaming and golden and clear.

The seer stepped forward, and chose a new path.

When the blue fist shot forward, she was already out of the way. Cotton spun around the tent rope and slid under a nearby wagon. The seer tucked and rolled, letting the momentum carry her all the way past the wagon to a yellow-brick wall where two merchants cowered. The black drill ripped through the wagon seconds later. Without pausing, Cotton pulled one of the merchants to his feet and pushed him into the oncoming drill. His screams and his blood spattered everywhere -- but not her screams, not her blood -- not on this path.

She ducked under a table and pulled the green cloth that covered it into her hands. Bronze rings and imitation gold jewelry slid off the top and clattered on the clay street. Cotton could track every one of them, knew where every one would fall.

The back of the blue machine was visible: the dusty glass cockpit, tiny arms moving frantically inside, whipping the drill back and forth seeking her. The spray of blood obscured the pilot's vision, as expected.

The seer dashed across the street, her feet landing in the perfect places. She tossed the green table cloth across the top of the cockpit. A scream of frustration came from within -- an odd chittering cry.

The cockpit sat on top of the engine, an endlessly writhing series of gears, levers and ornate flanges. Cotton plunged her hand between the gears and grabbed a small knob, nearly obscured by the rest of the mechanism. She did not cry out as the heat seared her palm and the twisting snapped three of her finger bones. This path required it, and a healer could repair the damage later.

The glass canopy popped open, taking a long, lazy arc through the air before shattering against the side of a building. Cotton pulled herself up, locked both legs around the small leather seat back, and grabbed the pilot's throat.

The pilot was a small brown bunny. Of course.

"Your Emperor grows foolhardy -- wasting the lives of his warriors needlessly. The book will be returned when I have completed my studies, and not a moment before." She held the rabbit by the scruff of its neck and pushed the kill switch on the machine's console. The blue fist and drill shuddered to a halt as she stepped off, her assailant dangling from her uninjured hand. The yellow blaze vanished from her eyes, like the door of a furnace quickly shut.

"Now, go." Cotton deposited the rabbit on the clay and gave it a quick push with her foot. It was gone at top speed, back down the hole it had emerged from.

The seer recovered her cloak, ignoring the stunned looks and whispers from the market crowd. She wrapped her broken hand as tightly as possible in the folds and moved back into the center of Gorah towards the library. She had hoped to spend the afternoon completing her translation of an Arkanic tablet, but she would need to have her hand looked at.

Linus was sitting on the steps. The broad yellow stone steps, the edges round and worn with years of wind.

A little grayer -- a lot thinner, a ghost -- his face angled up towards the afternoon sun, his eyes closed.

Cotton made herself breathe and approach.

The seer hated surprises. They were an affront to her occupation and skill. And a visit from the aged knight was a very unpleasant one.

Dull-gray armor without adornment -- she had never seen him without it. He had removed his gauntlets, and they lay neatly at his side. His slender fingers knit around his right knee as he smiled up at a passing sparrow. Linus the Spellbreaker seemed completely at peace.

A wave of pain from her injured hand. Cotton realized she had been clenching her broken fist and forced herself to relax. She stepped closer and willed her voice to sound calm.

"What do you want, old man?"

His eyes popped open -- faded green, like dying moss. "Ah, my child. What a pleasure to see you again. Encounter some trouble?"

His eyes indicated her bundled hand.

"Spare me your false concern -- nothing I couldn't handle. I am on my way to have a healer tend to my hand. Magical healing is expensive, but within my means." *Shut up, shut up. You're already talking to much, accounting for your actions. It's none of his affair.*

"I am glad to hear that. You will need to be at peak condition for the task ahead."

"Task."

"Yes, Cotton Belaine. A task that requires your skills, your training, and your obedience."

The seer brushed past the gray knight. *How dare he speak as if no time had passed, as if this was commonplace, as if he had the right?*

"Cotton," he said. "It's a wild mage."

She stopped.

"I'll have my hand repaired and be ready to ride at dawn."

From many paths to one, the seer went into the library and did not look back.

8

Jonas jabbed his hand down into the pool. He felt his fingernails brush against the cavefish's scales, but it darted away. Again.

The squire grunted with frustration. He ran both hands through his curly hair and pulled for a moment, eyes-wide staring up at the waterfall. Jonas breathed deeply and tried to swallow his irritation.

He shivered in the cold water and looked down into the pool as the ripples subsided.

"Are you laughing at me, fish?" he asked. "You and your fish-friends?"

In the past hour he had named the four fish that lived in the pool. Fat One, Blue One, Skinny One, and Spotty One. It was Blue One that had dodged his last attempt.

"Well, I'm going to catch one of you. One of you is going to be eaten. By me." Jonas pointed accusingly at Blue One, then back at himself.

"Why are you talking to fish?" Rime said quietly.

92

SPELL/SWORD

Jonas wheeled around in surprise, splashing water and scattering the fish to the far edges of the pool. The mage was still seated on her stool. The only movement she had made was to raise her head up from her chest.

"Because... because... I thought..well..." he made a vague gesture towards the pool and started walking towards the edge to cover his embarrassment.

The mage's lips twitched in what could have been a smile - - then she saw the black tattoo on the squire's goose-pimpled chest.

Three swords bound inside a circle. The mark was on his right breast, just under the collarbone.

Jonas pulled himself onto the bank, icy water dripping off him. He hopped from foot to foot, trying to stay warm as he struggled back into his shirt.

"You're from Gilead," the mage said.

The squire stopped, head and arms still lost in the folds of cloth. "What makes you say that?"

"The tattoo on your chest. It's the mark of the Iron Legion. Founded 860 AV, by Galvin the Wise. Principal military might of the country of Gilead. Also known as the White Crusaders, the Sword of the Faith. Primarily infantry, with the officer corps comprised of four chivalric orders. You are a deserter."

The boy hadn't moved. Rime sighed.

"Could you please finish putting your shirt on? It's like I'm talking to a giant pillow-monster."

93

Jonas slowly pulled his shaggy head through the neck of the shirt and looked up slowly. His expression was blank.

"You are old enough to have enlisted, but too young to have been honorably retired. You are a proficient fighter, which shows some degree of military training. You are not wounded, so you couldn't have been relieved of duty. You are clearly too unskilled to be off on some sort of assignment alone. You were imprisoned in Talbot for a drunken brawl, which suggests a low moral character. You have displayed a bent towards a chivalric honor code, however, offering downed foes a chance to yield, reluctance to kill an unarmed opponent. Conclusion: You are a deserter. You ran away and fled across the sea." Rime stood up as she finished.

"Or," Jonas said slowly. "Or I just have a tattoo."

Rime scoffed. "Why did you run away?"

The squire began to pull methodically on his boots. He tucked the soaked ends of his breeches into the top of each boot.

"Why did you run away?" the mage repeated.

Jonas looked up.

"Where are we going? Why are we in such a hurry? Why are you travelling alone? Why take such a risk, when your power is so dangerous?"

Rime opened her mouth to reply, then closed it into a tight frown.

Jonas stood up, and moved over to the bundled blanket

SPELL/SWORD

and pulled out a hunk of bread. He tore it in half and tossed one portion over to the mage.

The two travellers did not speak while they ate. After a time they both went to their bed rolls.

"Do you know how to play chess?"

Rime said nothing.

Jonas leaned his head up. "Hey, Rime. Do you know how to play chess?"

The small bump of dark that was the mage's body turned obstinately away.

"I mean, I figured you would. Know how to play. Just seems like the sort of thing you'd know how to do." He leaned his head back against the cold stone floor. " I don't know why I was thinking about it, but I used to play chess all the time. Then I was trying to remember when the last time I played was, and where I was."

Jonas did his best to pull the brown cloak a little tighter around himself, eyes staring up into the sunflower-yellow light that illuminated the cave ceiling.

"I'm sure this is boring you. Is this boring you, Rime?"

The bump of dark constricted and said nothing.

A few moments passed. The squire stared up at the cave ceiling, but did not see it. His voice was quiet when he spoke again.

"I guess the last time I played was with Master. He was so good. He would just smoke his pipe and make his moves

95

right away. Wouldn't even pause while he was talking, kept on telling me about different kinds of shields, or the proper way to treat a harness after a snowstorm, or the smell that a wound has when it's festered. Sliding the pieces like he knew from the beginning where each one would go."

Jonas chuckled.

"Not me, though. I would stare at the board forever. I'd pick up a piece, look up at him, put it down. Pick up another piece, squint between the rows, look back up at him, hoping to get a clue. Nothing, not a nod, not a wink. I never won. Not one single time. I never even came close."

"Then... "the mage sighed with exasperation, without unfolding her body or turning towards the squire. "Then why did you keep playing? What's the point if you never win?"

"I liked the pieces. Bright, polished marble. The little knobby soldiers, and the horse-head knights best of all. I never got the hang of the bishops, and Master would take my queen right away. Said it was a 'mercy' – 'like taking a sharp blade away from a child'. Oh, and the towers with the weird name..."

"Rooks."

"Yeah, those. You should've seen the set Master had. It was heavy wood, and dark -- a box with steel clasps. But then it folded open, and each piece was fit in its own velvet nook. Master brought it everywhere we traveled, and every night he'd send me to get it from his things, and set it up near the fire for us to play."

"So." Rime's sneer was palpable. "You enjoyed losing the same game over and over because it came in a pretty box, and the pieces were shiny. Unsurprising."

"It wasn't like that," Jonas grumbled. "It was... Never mind, you wouldn't understand."

"Uh-huh." The mage sounded smug.

Time and quiet stretched out between them. He felt the anger in his stomach twist and burn, then finally begin to cool. He waited until he was sure he could hear her faint snores before he let himself finish his argument. It was the only way he would get the final word, he figured.

"It was that the game was fair. The pieces are right in front of you, and so are the rules. No surprises, no cheats, no dodges. And it was always possible to win. Maybe this time. Maybe this time..."

Rime woke up first. The yellow light shone steadily from behind the waterfall, and a quiet roar filled her ears. She blinked once and did not move.

It was a rare moment. Her mind was empty and she had dreamed of nothing. The mage listened to the water and tried to hold on to the emptiness.

A red line appeared, skittering across her vision. A thought. It hungrily sketched out several geometric shapes and began to fill one corner with a dim web of ideas. A blue circle bloomed in the center, irising open cleanly as roses never do. The circle spun, then budded, smaller blue orbs appearing on its perimeter. An orange line dashed in from the left, calculating the trajectory of each orb.

Notations were sketched by a bright white triangle, numbers and words; four languages for each footnote. Four green bars dropped into view, and after providing a brief obstacle for the orange line, settled into a sturdy square.

The red web continued to spin. The other thoughts avoided it with practiced ease.

Rime did not sigh. The red thoughts were taking up more and more territory. She cocked an eyebrow and zeroed in on something new.

A brown thought. A stodgy line, moving slowly as a brushstroke. It seemed to be trapped in one quadrant of her mind, careening drunkenly in a tiny space. It moved forward, then would reverse, move forward then reverse. It had nowhere to go, but refused to stop moving.

She stood up and kicked Jonas' boots. He snorted, and opened his eyes. He looked around wildly, then focused on her.

"Wha--? Why the kick? I'm up."

"Let's go. We've wasted enough time." Rime walked away towards the three exits that led from the chamber.

Jonas pushed the hair out of his face and gathered their meager provisions. He uncovered the two crystal torches and put his sword belt back on. The combination of the green and yellow light made the red cotton of his shoulder strap appear washed out and strange.

The three exits waited. Two stone-carved doorways and a narrow mine-shaft leading into darkness. The squire had pretty much lost any sense of direction during their

SPELL/SWORD

journey underground, but he thought that the mine-shaft led in a more northerly direction. He handed one torch to the mage. Rime moved forward, inspecting the carvings in the crisp green light of the torch.

Kort mind-var. Grad. Kort mind-var. Begrosh. "Tunnels Four and Seven," she said. "And the one we came out of was Six."

Jonas spun in a slow circle, angling his torch into the darker corners of the chamber. He stopped and leaned into the first part of the rough shaft.

"Is this Five, then?"

"Unlikely. Dwarven engineers would not go out of sequence like that. All of the main tunnels should radiate out from a central hub. If we follow either one of these, we should find the hub and access to the surface." Rime's voice was distant, her mind's eye watching the rainbow lines of her ideas converge and chart out the solution, extrapolating the possible routes that would lead her to the mine's center.

"How do you know all that?"

The lines screeched to a halt and spun in annoyed gyres. The brown blotch in her mind merrily continued to bump against a cerulean thought.

"Books. Lots of them," she replied. "Let's go."

The squire sighed and managed a dry chuckle.

"You're the boss," he said to her back and the vanishing torchlight. Rime moved down Tunnel Seven and did not look back.

99

"Bye, fish. Next time," she heard the squire promise, followed by the sound of thin-leather boots as he trotted after her.

The tunnel curved gently to the right, then straightened for nearly a half mile. The squire and mage passed briefly through a small chamber that seemed to be devoted to repair work. Several dusty carts were piled in a corner next to a brace of broken axles. A new tunnel branched off to the right, but Rime continued on her course without even pausing. Jonas took a half-hearted glance down the new tunnel, but once again found no reason to doubt the mage's judgment. He had to move quickly over the broken boards and stone axles to catch up with his companion. Rime turned suddenly to the left wall, and the squire skipped out of the way to avoid a collision.

The mage ran her fingers carefully through a patch of thick moss growing on the tunnel wall. It was thick and peltlike, appearing almost a dark purple in the green torchlight. The books in her head flew open and settled on the appropriate page. She nodded and turned to continue down the tunnel only to discover the brown-cloaked squire leaning in her path.

"Look, I get that you are sick of questions, but I don't like being in the dark. I can tell you learned something from the moss-petting. How about you just tell me and save me asking five to fifteen annoying questions?"

"Fine. Keep walking, then," Rime said.

Jonas obliged.

100

SPELL/SWORD

"It's Webster's Carpet, a pretty common moss of no special use or notice. It needs direct sunlight to grow. This patch is struggling, but it must connect to a healthier colony. It couldn't survive more than a few dozen feet below ground. It means we're near the surface."

Rime stopped walking. The green torchlight was being steadily supplanted by natural light coming from the tunnel ahead. She removed the glowing shard from the end of the torch, and tossed the splintered board aside. It clattered against the stone floor. The mage tucked the crystal in her belt for further study, and waited for the squire to catch up.

"You go in first," she instructed.

Jonas grimaced and placed his crystal torch on the floor. It made perfect sense, again. They were getting close to the exit, the chance of danger increased -- the mage would be most effective if he and his sword kept any attackers at bay, especially since the chamber ahead seemed to be of significant size. It was a perfectly sound battle-plan.

But a barb dug into his stomach. She had put it all together so swiftly. No doubt, no discussion. The clearest, best plan while he was still staring at the board. *Just like Master...*

Jonas drew his sword and pushed the irritation and memory aside. He stepped into the larger chamber that was flooded with early morning sunshine.

A turtle-shell made of glass was the roof of the chamber. Thick, hexagonal panes deftly connected by broad channels of stone and brass. The light refracted slightly through dense spirals and whorls etched on each massive pane. The squire lowered his sword in wonder.

Rime leaned carefully around the stone door frame. The squire was goggling at the ceiling. "Apparently, this chamber is secure," she said.

Jonas scratched his head, engrossed in the glass dome. The mage moved a few paces into the chamber and looked around slowly. She wasted no energy chastising her bodyguard.

The chamber was almost completely circular. Six tunnels departed this room, including the one Rime had just exited. The portals were cleanly chiseled with Dwarven runes. In the center of the room was a giant bronze screw. It was as broad as a house, and the top of it nearly touched the turtle-shell dome. The metal spiralling up the sides served as a broad walkway, and the mage could clearly see cunning doorways set at regular intervals up the ramp. The rest of the chamber was in serious disarray, filled with knocked over carts and piles of pitchstone left unsorted.

The mage's mind summoned phantom figures to move around the room, imagining the final moments this place was occupied. She made the imaginary dwarves a bright orange and gave each of them an elaborate headlamp. She almost placed candles inside their lanterns, but instead put glowing green crystals. The crystals had formed long after this place was abandoned, but it looked nice in her mind's eye.

One phantom held up a bent shovel. The wooden handle was pitted and worn. *Poor working conditions.*

Another dwarf-image moved towards a rusted water-trough and tugged at a metal cup. The cup was chained to the side of the basin. *They didn't trust the workers.* A pair of phantoms grabbed clubs and began to cruelly beat a third. Rime turned slowly towards the giant screw, and focused on the lowest door. A group of phantoms huddled around the door, as one hammered away at the lock with a pickaxe. *A riot, a worker's rebellion.*

The throng of dwarves created by her mind beat their way up the spiral staircase, bashing their way into door after door. They carried strange, square tokens and tossed them over the side. Rime leaned over and pulled one out of the dirt. She brushed it off, and read the faded script stamped into the iron token. *Ephraim Mining - 10 ptoch.*

"How do we get out... maybe up the ramp?" Jonas' voice broke in on her thoughts.

Rime dismissed the orange phantoms and started up the bronze screw's spiral stair.

9

The dawn light shone through the thick glass. The dome was only a few inches above their heads -- a comfortable distance for its dwarven engineers, but Jonas had little difficulty reaching up to run his finger along the strange whorls in the surface of the glass. The squire guessed that the glass had to be nearly a foot thick. Jonas ducked his head, then neatly tripped over a large raised rune on the floor. The squire landed hard on his palms, and barked his left shin.

"Good thing you finally put away your sword," Rime remarked, not looking back.

The top of the screw reminded Jonas of the face of a clock, the raised runes connected by fine silver etchings twisted and knotted around each rune. Rime sank to her knees and inspected several of the runes with fierce concentration.

Jonas picked himself up and checked his shin. The skin was unbroken, but a nasty purple bruise was forming

SPELL/SWORD

gleefully. On their way up the stairs, they had carefully checked each of the doors that weren't locked shut. He had entered the first two with sword drawn, but found only empty rooms, rubble and dust. Rime sniffed each time and pushed his sword arm out of her way, and had surveyed each room. The only thing they found of any interest was a pair of Dwarf skeletons, dry and covered with filth.

The squire tucked the pant leg back into his boot and moved carefully around the perimeter of the screw-top. The chamber had no obvious exits, some scaffolding twenty feet distant that led off towards other tunnels, but nothing that seemed to lead out to where the dawn sun shone. The only thing of interest was an elaborate bronze disc at the very center of the turtle-glass dome. A bold rune made from inset glass glowed at the center of the disc. Jonas scratched his cheek and waited patiently for the mage to explain to him what the rune said.

And waited.

Don't look over there, Jonas. Don't even ask. Just keep staring at the dome, the squire counseled himself.

Another minute passed.

He turned his head slightly to catch the mage in the corner of his eye.

Rime was sitting in the exact same place, running her hands across the etchings. Her eyes wide, as if she was looking at a grand tapestry and trying to find the one single thread that bound it all together.

That is one great dome, Jonas. Just keep looking at it....

The squire craned his head a bit more.

The mage had turned her back to him, following the strange pattern of the silver lines on the floor.

Jonas sighed. "Umm... what..."

"It says 'Exit'. Somehow these runes can be used to open it. Now, shut up," Rime said.

Jonas stood for a moment, one hand still extended to point towards the bronze disc. He closed his mouth slowly and sat on the edge of a reasonably square rune.

It was going to be a long day.

"Wake up."

Jonas shook his head. He felt hot, grimy sweat on the back of his neck. The sun had moved, and it was just past noon. The turtle-glass dome shone brightly under the direct sunlight. Rime was standing a few paces away.

"I know how to open the dome, but I need your assistance," she continued.

The squire stood up and wiped his palms on the edge of his brown cloak. He checked his sword and looked up at the wild mage.

"Okay, what do you need me to do?" he said.

"Dance."

SPELL/SWORD

"Um, what?"

Rime spoke very distinctly. "Dance. Do you know how to dance?"

"Sure, I've danced. At festivals, and the like..." Jonas spread his hands awkwardly and took a few steps towards the girl.

"What are you doing?"

Jonas stopped in his tracks, hands held out. "Oh, you didn't mean for me... for you..."

"No." Rime turned and moved to the center of the screwtop. "These runes are simple words and phrases in the dwarven language. Up. Down. Cloud. Rain. Fire. Water. Tree. Seed. Stone. Hammer. Mug. Bread."

She pointed out each rune as she passed.

"The top of this screw tower is a lock. It's designed for four dwarves to press the correct runes in sequence, after you press the central pad to begin. In Pergunter Max's *Travels and Travails,* he makes mention of witnessing a similar device in the dwarven vaults of Styr. He called them a 'dance-lock'. This device is clearly much more contemporary, but the principle should be the same. I can't run fast enough to do it myself, but it should be feasible for the two of us to enter the sequence."

"So... what?" Jonas pointed around the rim of the screwtop. "We just run around and stomp on the runes in the right order?"

"Yes." Rime turned back to face the squire.

107

"Wait. How do we know what the right order is?"

"The spiral staircase we climbed. A sequence of runes is etched on the underside. This is clearly the sequence to open the dome," Rime explained.

Jonas stared at her for a moment.

"What? Don't you ever look up?" Rime said.

The squire rubbed his face with both hands and took a long breath.

"The sequence is thirty-two characters. I have studied the layout of the runes on the floor extensively, and the two of us should be able to move quickly enough to activate all of them in time. There should be a delay of a few seconds between each, allowing us to cover the distance between. The runes in the tunnels were Common Syprian, but these are High Dwarven. Can you memorize these symbols?" Rime continued.

Jonas laughed and nodded briskly.

"Of course you can't," Rime sighed.

The sun had moved a few more finger-lengths before they were ready to begin. The mage had stormed back down the spiral staircase and returned several minutes later with an armful of green crystal and black clay. Methodically, she marked sixteen runes. Each one received a chip of glowing crystal and a broad number scrawled on the brass floor.

"You can count, right?" she asked.

Jonas summoned the most dignified expression he could muster and nodded. The squire carefully walked the path he would need to make. The longest stretches were between 5 and 6, 9 and 10; 13,14, and 15 were almost on opposite sides of the screwtop.

Rime said nothing until he completed his survey. She stood at the center of the screwtop and watched his careful tread.

"You have half the runes, and I have half. We'll be alternating -- taking turns, you step on one, then I have the next, and so on. Do you understand? There won't be time for questions once we begin," the mage said as Jonas came towards the center.

Once more, Jonas was amazed at how quickly the young girl's mind worked. No wasted effort, smooth and quick. *Like a machine.*

The squire went and stood next to the rune marked with a '1'. He slung the red strap of his sword around his chest and bent his knees, angling himself towards the second rune.

"Do you go first, or do I?" he said.

"I do," Rime said and stomped down hard on the center pad with both feet.

There was a dusky click as the pad sank slightly.

A vast clamor of creaking gears and squealing metal filled the cavern. Jonas looked around wildly, and saw that the edge of the screwtop was moving slowly. Panels slid open coughing dust, and strange tubes emerged and craned

109

outwards into the air.

Slow and quiet, the forgotten trumpets began to play. The music had a stately rhythm, reminding the two travelers of a king's march mixed with a fiddler's reel.

"Pay attention!" the wild mage shouted. "A new rune must be pressed at the start of each musical phrase, every three measures!"

Jonas saw the slim girl push hard on the first rune, and he placed a foot on his first mark. The beat of the song was easy to follow, and he pressed the stone pad down hard when his time came.

The squire immediately trotted over to the second mark. Rime was still dashing across the central pad making her way to her next target.

From somewhere in the bowels of the dance-lock, a chorus of dwarven voices began to sing.

Making money, honey -- way down in the ground. Spend it all up on you when we get to town.

A slight distortion to the voices made it clear they were hearing some long-forgotten recording. Jonas pressed hard on his second rune and ran towards the third. He had to jump to the side suddenly when his path neatly intersected Rime's.

"Don't step on the wrong runes!" the young girl yelled, already out of breath.

The squire looked down and saw he had one toe on an unmarked rune. Jonas swallowed and continued on.

Bottom of the glass, then I'll pinch your ass and dance around the town.... the recorded dwarves bellowed.

He barely made it to the third rune with a few breaths to spare. Glancing at Rime, he saw her press another rune and immediately dash off to her next target. She was slowing down, her face running with sweat.

"Are you all right?" he called. " You look a little -- crap." Jonas kicked off the next rune just in time and ran on.

...and the copper's on fire, and the green-smoke mire, and I just want to go way back down.

The two moved through the next several runes in the sequence without incident, but Jonas could see that the mage was visibly slowing with each sprint. Rime had to step twice on her twelfth rune before it clicked into place, then pushed damp hair out of her face and staggered forward.

"Way back down, beneath the ground, digging for the boss man's fee. Making money, honey -- making money, honey!"

Jonas ran full speed across the central pedal to make his next goal but kept his head towards the mage as he yelled. "Hey! Are you going to be okay? Come on, we're almost done!"

"Shut up." Rime gasped and lunged forward, nearly tripping in her exhaustion.

The recorded dwarves grew louder and more jubilant as the finale of the song arrived, repeating the same verse again and again. Rime's knees buckled as she fell forward onto her rune.

"Are you okay?" Jonas called. He was on the far opposite side of the dance-lock.

Money, honey -- money, money -- money, honey -- spend it all on you in town...

"Shut up," the weak response came.

Jonas was panting slightly as he made his way to the next rune. There were only two left to go. He was worried about the girl's health, but he knew he had to focus on the task at hand. Imagining the mage's anger if he missed his count made him grin.

Out of the corner of his eye, he saw her erupt. The dusty dwarven chorus rattled on unconcerned.

Rime was encased in a blazing red nimbus of energy. She shot across the screwtop towards her next goal like a meteor. Jonas stared with his mouth open and stopped moving. The mage rotated swiftly around in her cloak of fire and caught his eye. Her hair was rippling up and down in the currents of her magic. Her voice seemed a thousand miles away.

"Don't just stand there. Move." She broke off and blazed across to her final rune.

The squire shook his head and moved to press the rune marked "16."

The jubilant song came to a close. The squire turned and faced the center of the dial, where Rime still hovered in red flame. The screwtop turned ever so slightly to the left.

The giant panes of thick, colored glass opened outwards, like the petals of a flower, leaving one still connected to the center of the dome. The central disc rose and locked into the underside of the petal. Thick bars popped out the side, making a simple staircase. Jonas breathed deeply, trying to catch his breath.

That was when he saw the fire-encased mage rocketing towards him.

She stopped bare inches from his side, close enough that he could feel the piercing heat of her aura. Through the flames he could see that her eyes were filled with white light. Her eyelids and face were taut with strain.

"Carry me out of here," she said.

Rime released her magic and collapsed to the floor.

Jonas sighed. "Okay."

10

The mage dreamed.

A thin-faced man stood in front of the room, flower petals spilling from his sleeves. They were lily petals, and Rime could see that the edges of each petal had been carefully cut, tiny triangles and half-moon shapes.

"Doma Korvanus, stand on the red box," he said, a worm crawling from his collar and across his face.

The room was filled with desks. She sat at one, with her hands folded in front of her on a blank sheet of paper. An ink-brush sat in a clay cup at the top corner of the desk. An ink-stone shaped like a teardrop lay alongside.

"The red box, Rime. The red box," her tutor droned, a note of irritation warming his voice.

Rime looked left and right. There was no red box.

SPELL/SWORD

A slow herd of wooden pigs walked across her field of vision, making a barrier between her and the instructor. Each of the pigs had a bright steel nose ring, and their left ears jangled with even more steel.

"The red box. Rime. Get on the red box."

"No," she replied.

The pigs squealed, and she looked down at her paper. It was no longer blank. A long black streak marred one half of the page. She looked at the ink-brush, it was still dripping. She held up her left hand; the fingertips were damp with ink.

"Rime, get on the red box. The red box, Doma. Doma!" Her tutor was becoming angry. Vicious tusks sprouted from his face, and she felt the bamboo cane hit her back, a familiar line of pain. This was wrong. He had been dead for years, and no one beat her any more. She made sure of that.

She looked back down at the paper. Two more slashes had appeared, and her left hand was black with ink. Was it a word? She stared at the slashes, trying to make sense of them.

"Doma Rime! Doma Rime! The red box!" The bamboo cane hit her again, but the instructor's voice seemed suddenly far away. She looked up.

The front of the classroom was stretching away from her as the pigs complacently snuffled between the desks. A wind began to blow from behind her; automatically she slapped a hand down on the desk to keep her paper from blowing away.

115

She looked down. Black letters had been scrawled on the paper. *J-O-N-A*. One final letter was obscured by her hand.

Very slowly she lifted her head and saw one of the pigs approach. It put its trotters up on the desk and opened its mouth wide. Caught between its yellow tusks was a mirror.

Rime looked at her own reflection and saw that her hair had turned white as snow.

She screamed.

Rime sat up, pushing brown fabric off her arms and onto the ground. She was propped against the trunk of a tree, and the orange hue of the sun told her that it was near sundown.

Jonas was sitting several paces away with his sword across his knees. He rose immediately when she stirred and began to walk across the clearing. She stared at him a moment. Something was different. Then she saw the answer was in her hands.

He's not wearing his cloak. He put his cloak over me.

Rime forced herself up and blearily tossed the cloak towards the approaching squire. He caught it and tucked the misshapen bundle under his arm as he approached.

"You feeling better?"

"I'm fine. How long has it been? Three hours?" she asked briskly.

"Closer to four. I carried you about half a mile into these

116

SPELL/SWORD

woods. I figured we should get as far away from the dome as we could before nightfall. It might have attracted the attention of those frog guys." Jonas pulled the cloak over his head in a practiced motion.

Not a complete idiot, then. Rime glanced around the clearing. The trees were broad cedars, but gave no clue as to their present location.

"Did you see any landmarks? We need to figure out where we are," she said.

Jonas finished pulling his cloak on and furrowed his brow in thought.

"There was still some more canyon, leading off to the north, but it didn't look like too much. I headed due east... mostly... if that helps," he said.

"Mostly?" Rime replied, but her mind was already unrolling its map. She made a few red marks on the map, estimating the minimum and maximum distance they could be from the end of the canyon. Then she made a wide arc enclosing the maximum distance the squire could have carried her.

"Well, there was a stream I had to cross after we got into the tree line. That may have made me lose my bearings slightly... but that wasn't too long before I stopped walking," the squire said defensively.

"The river. It ran north to south? Which way was the water flowing?" Rime asked.

"South, I think." Jonas looked off towards the trees. "No, definitely south. I remember."

117

Her mind's quill drew a thin blue line parallel to the canyon. She continued the line north-east and found a larger river. Her careful study of all the maps in her father's library had resulted in a very exact mental map of this area. She was certain it was the Jericho River. She finished the thin blue line of the tributary and connected it to the Jericho. A red circle appeared where the two connected and was soon surrounded by a battalion of question marks. She swatted them aside, and they splashed into the blue ink of the larger river.

She had to be right. They were very low on supplies, and if the tributary lead them to the Jericho River, the village of Jericho was waiting a few hours north on the west bank.

"Come on, take me back to the stream. We can follow it north to the Jericho River. There's a village nearby where we can get some food." She straightened her clothes and pushed some stray hair out of her eyes. Remembering the dream, she felt comforted in seeing that it was the same light brown.

Jonas nodded in satisfaction and relief. He had spent the past two hours frantically trying to figure out what they should do next, and coming up with nothing. Rime was awake for less than two minutes, and she had already formed a sound plan. *I'm just a soldier, I guess.*

Rime began to limp out of the clearing towards the direction of the stream, exhaustion still clear on her face. Jonas started to reach out and take her elbow, but then he stopped. He had carried her for miles at her instruction, but he knew she would greet any other help with anger.

SPELL/SWORD

Hands off the general, Jonas.

The two travelers made their way out of the clearing.

The river was brown and wide, coffee-colored and completely uninteresting.

Crude, wooden palisades were the only defense the small town seemed to have, but large gaps had been left open between the structures. Spanning between were dozens of ropes and cords -- a rainbow of colors, different thicknesses and fabrics. A cord of blue silk, next to an oil-stained coil of cotton rope, next to a long strip of red leather. Jonas ran a hand along the cotton rope and held it up with one finger for Rime to see. He grunted quizzically. The mage narrowed her eyes, but ultimately shrugged. The squire let go of the cord with satisfaction. *Finally something she hasn't read about before.*

The two travelers' journey north had been as drab as the river. As they approached the river, the pine forest had quickly thinned into a land of gray rocks and green scrub. They had taken regular rest breaks at Jonas' insistence. He took it as a mark of Rime's exhaustion that she had not questioned him. The dark circles under her eyes were still prominent, but she seemed to be breathing easier as the afternoon wore on.

Beyond the palisades and ropes was a field of daffodils. A scant half mile further was the first of the wooden buildings that made up the simple village of Jericho.

Just beyond that was the bridge.

119

Jonas and Rime stopped and stared. It was like finding a flea-bitten donkey with a golden saddle.

The vast white bridge stretched nimbly across the brown waters of the river. It was smooth and straight, graceful archways connecting the sleek white pillars that supported it. From this distance, it appeared to be made of stone, but the supports were as light and graceful as if carved from birch.

"Precursor architecture," Rime said. "It must be."

"Pre-what-or?" Jonas replied.

The girl rolled her eyes and set out across the daffodils.

Rime eyed the buildings as she approached. Her mind's quill quickly catalogued the structures. *Fisherman. Fisherman. Tanner. Fisherman. Stable. Fisherman. Fisherman. Fisherman.*

"It's a fishing village," she said as Jonas tromped up behind her, hopefully forestalling any questions.

Looking out across the white bridge, she quickly spotted dozens of fishing lines hanging off it like dirty cobwebs. A handful of simple wooden boats made their way around the river casting nets. The late afternoon sun shimmered on the brown water. Rime estimated it would be at least an hour before the fishing boats finished for the day and rowed back into the village.

"So, what is our plan? We have a few bread crusts in the sack and fewer coins. And you are clearly in a hurry to complete your secret errand, so we don't have time to set up a sweet shop," the squire said, hitching a thumb into his sword belt.

The two were making their way past the first few buildings. All seemed empty. A wide muddy track lead into the center of the village. The murmur of conversation could be heard ahead, as well as the sharp notes of a flute.

Rime continued to appraise the rude wooden buildings they passed. *Fisherman. Fisherman. Baker. Fisherman. Seamstress.*

"Clearly a currency-poor township, most likely driven by barter. We need to trade something for the supplies we need," she said.

"What have we got to trade?" Jonas replied skeptically.

"Your sword."

Rime tried to fight from grinning at the absurdly possessive way he clutched at the bedraggled red strap of his weapon. She lost the fight.

The mage turned away from the squire with a lofty expression. Her bodyguard was right: they had precious little time and nothing to trade. Nothing physical at least.

Silver notes filled the air as the flute grew more audible. A voice joined in.

"Well away, through the fog and rain
and I'll never come back this way again.
Song and dance,
and backward glance,
my true love lost his final chance.

Well away, through the fog and rain..."

A busy marketplace sprawled out in the center of the village. The calls of fishmongers quickly accompanied the music. Various pavilions and rough stalls sat on smooth white stone, Rime quickly recognized that it was an ancient road that led east towards the bridge.

She leaned down and inspected the stone. Rime couldn't find a single crack in its surface or a blemish of dirt. The Precursor civilization fascinated her, referred to as the 'Arkanic' race in most scholarly texts. So little was known about them. They had vanished from the face of Aufero thousands of years ago. In their wake they left structures and devices of unparalleled complexity, durability and beauty. Many of the mechanical wonders that now existed were cribbed and copied from rediscovered Arkanic technology. Paper that never rotted, swords that sang, bells that spoke, a dam that turned salt water into fresh, extruding blocks of pressed white salt. Perfect and without need of repair. Like this bridge, thin columns white and clean for thousands of years, and now hundreds of dirty fishermen squatted here. Cleaning their daily catch of fish on the edge of the bridge, guts and blood everywhere. The mage felt a brief urge to push all of the shouting people off the white stone.

"..take heel and prance,
one backward glance –
My true love lost her final chance."

The singer was a portly wood elf, long red hair flowing over her thick shoulders and overstuffed bosom. She flared her skirt and spun around the flute player, a squat human woman with thick brown braids wound up in a bright green scarf. The Yad-Elf continued to spin as the

122

SPELL/SWORD

song ended, coming to rest in the outstretched arms of the flute. The two performers shared a wild kiss and bowed to a smattering of applause from the passing fishermen and traders.

Rime's mind spooled out a quick assessment. *Performers. Travelers. Bards. Source of information.*

The mage pushed past a pair of dark-haired children reeking of fish and approached the two performers.

"You'll need to watch your arpeggios, love," the wood elf said, straightening the collar of the human woman. "You're starting to drag."

"It's not my flute playing, it's those silly boots you wear. Heavier than stones, making you miss the beat," the woman replied, tucking her flute into a long pocket stitched on the side of her leggings.

"Don't start in again about the boots -- they accentuate my calves, and I got them for a song."

"A song and more, to that granny-tanner in Falcreek... don't think I don't remember. You smiled and flounced for nearly an hour before..."

"Good evening," Rime interrupted.

The two bards broke off their argument and nodded to each other. The well-worn discussion was smoothly placed back on the shelf. They turned as one and bowed grandly to the young girl.

"And a wonderful evening to you as well, mistress," the wood elf said. "My name is Canteen, and my partner is

123

Larabell. We've been in Jericho for a pile of days, but this is our first meeting, so you must be a traveler like us!"

"My name is Rime. And yes, I have been travelling," The wild mage grimaced. She despised conversation.

"Oh, how wonderful. Perhaps she'll have a fine tale to add to our store, Larabell!" Canteen cooed and spun in place.

Larabell grunted.

The mage eyed the brown-haired woman. *I wonder if I can talk to this one instead?*

"Oh, is this your young man I see trotting up?" The fat dancer pointed.

"My young... what?" Rime turned and looked behind her.

Jonas was disentangling himself from a pair of small boys, both clearly fixated on the squire's sword. He pulled the sword's scabbard from their awed hands and slung it back over his shoulder with a grin.

"I like his hair," Larabell said. "Big floppy sheep-dog."

"Big hands, too," Canteen added. "You're quite the lucky one, Mistress Rime."

Rime assembled a blistering reply in her mind, then decided to hold her tongue.

The two bards bowed gracefully as the squire came close, and Jonas managed a passable half-bow in return.

"It's a pleasure to meet you two ladies," he said with mothball courtesy. Someone had taught the young man

SPELL/SWORD

how to bow, but the gesture had been kept far back in the closet.

"Oh the pleasure is ours, kind sir. Canteen and Larabell, Troubadours -- at your service," the dancer cooed.

"My name is Jonas of...Jonas." he replied.

"Jonas of Jonas?" The flute-player raised an eyebrow.

"Huh… just Jonas," he said.

"We were just speaking with your lady here and wondering what fine tales your travels have spun," Canteen gestured grandly towards Rime.

"My... what?" Jonas said looking towards the mage.

"Supplies. We need them. Blacksmith. Where is it? General information about the city and the surrounding area. Do you have any? And the Wheelbrake." Rime's words fell upon the awkward moment like a barrage, and her glance neatly kicked the squire in the gut.

Canteen chuckled and bowed to the stern-faced girl.

"So forward! Can't you buy a girl a drink first?

11

"And then we fought some frog guys, and got lost in a cave -- and then we had to do some weird dance thing to open the door -- how'd that song go, Rime? -- Money, money -- honey, honey! Money, money, money, money!"

Jonas was drunk.

Rime sat on her hands to keep from throttling him, and leaned across the splintered wooden table towards the two bards. They were listening intently to the squire's story, nodding at all the appropriate moments. She thought about the lack of gold in her pocket and the cost of the cheap bottle of alcohol that Jonas was swilling.

"I think that's enough of our story for the moment. Now, how about some of my questions?" she demanded.

"Oh let him finish the song, mistress," Canteen grinned.

SPELL/SWORD

"It's one of Larabell's favorites, an old Dwarven drinking chantey. We have to sing it three times a night when we go through Sypria."

The squat flute player rolled her eyes and raised a mug to her lips.

"Dah-duhn, duhn--doo doo" the drunk squire extemporized. He laughed, spraying ale across the table. Jonas slammed his mug down, then stared at it. He picked up the mug again and tapped it against the wooden plank enjoying the sound that it made.

A flare of laughter from a nearby table, a joke about the romantic aspirations of shepherds.

The screech of chair-legs as three fat fishermen cleared floor space for a game of dice. The dice were elaborately woven from tiny fish bones.

Rime pressed two fingers of each hand into her forehead as a headache hatched. Her hands, realizing they were free from their temporary prison, slowly reached across the table towards Jonas, making choking movements.

Canteen smoothly grabbed the mage's grasping hands and pulled her back towards the center of the table. The squire continued to tap his mug on the table rhythmically and hum, chin on his breastbone.

"Don't fret, child. You two have had a hard road, and in between the off-key warbling, your young man tells a stirring tale." Canteen twirled a strand of red hair around a thick finger. "More than worth a bottle of horse piss or two on our tab."

The bard rubbed the girl's hands kindly and winked. Rime

127

glowered, sickened by her feeling of relief.

"He is not 'my young man,' and I am not a child. I have business to attend to, and can easily get coin if you will answer my questions. My time is short, and I need to get to my destination," she said.

"To Wheelbrake?" Larabell said. "Let's talk about that a moment."

The mage grimaced and tried to pull her hands free from Canteen's thick fingers. The bard's grip tightened, not unkindly.

Jonas continued to tap his mug on the table, letting his head loll back.

"That's a nasty, perilous place, Mistress Rime. You aren't planning on going there, are you?" Canteen whispered. "Please tell me you aren't."

"That's none of your concern."

"It is my concern. And Larabell's concern. And this boy's concern. And everyone in this inn, the streets of Jericho, and all the little fishes in the water. Going to Wheelbrake is a 'road paved in bones,' as my old granny used to say."

"Dog-eared adages from your grandmother aside, could you just tell me where the blacksmith is? I have business with him, then I can repay your generosity."

"Generosity? Rime, I can't say this enough, that place is dangerous! Haven't you heard the tales, the dark songs? What could compel a slip of a thing like you to trudge the weary miles to that swamp?"

SPELL/SWORD

Jonas toppled backwards in his chair, laughing uproariously. "Don't ask, she'll never tell you--"

His head made a significant thud on the floor, and the squire fell silent. Canteen glanced away from the severe girl for a moment to check that he was still breathing, but did not release her grip on Rime's hands.

"Let me tell you a tale about the Wheelbrake Marsh. The perils, the dangers, the malevolent evils..." the bard began, elongating each word for emphasis.

"Nope," Larabell interrupted.

Canteen rolled her eyes and hissed out of the side of her mouth. "Excuse me? This is an incredibly dramatic moment, and you are spoiling it."

"I tell the stories."

"Not nearly as well as I do!"

The flute player reached over and thumped the pink-rosy lobe of Canteen's left ear.

"Ow!"

"I tell the stories?" Larabell thumped her partner's ear again.

"Ow! Stop that!"

"I tell the stories?" Thump.

"Ow! Yes, you tell the stories! You greasy cow!"

129

Thump. "Good."

Larabell raised the steel flute to her lips and blew a few slow notes. Rime pried her hands loose from the red-haired bard and shook the blood back into them. The mage was irritated by the new delay, but information on her destination could be useful. *Still wishing I'd watched my tongue a little more closely.*

The flute trilled an expectant melody, and a few of the fishermen nearby leaned in close to listen. Larabell held her flute up as a baton, and gathered the moment of silence around her.

"Once upon a time..."

"Story time?!" Jonas yelled. The squire leaned his elbow on the table, and pulled his head up to rest next to the mostly empty bottle. He held the back of his head and winced, smiling happily at Larabell. Canteen patted his head.

Larabell played another trill and began.

Once upon a time, there were three brothers. Slow Jack, Fast Jack, and Strong Jack. Their father was a shepherd and his flocks were small, but healthy and strong.

The three boys grew up in the green fields of Carroway, tending to their father's sheep. Whenever a sheep fell ill, Strong Jack would toss the wooly beast over his shoulders and carry them back to the fold. Whenever a wolf was spotted, Fast Jack would run faster than the wind to warn his brothers to come protect the flock. Whenever a plan had to be made, Slow Jack would close his eyes and sit

130

SPELL/SWORD

down on a rock and think and think, until the grass grew up beside his boots. Then his eyes would pop open and he'd calmly explain his idea.

Those were happy times, but one day their father fell ill.

He called his sons to his bedside and kissed them tenderly on their brows.

"My sons..." he began. "Death waits for me to journey with him, and I can only stall for so long. You've worked hard and been good sons, so when I die, I want you to split my herds, fairly and evenly among you and go out into the world to seek your fortune."

The brothers wept and promised they would. That very night Death quietly slipped in, helped himself to a spare mutton pie, and whisked their father away.

The next day, the three brothers rose and prepared to leave on their own journey. Each put on his travelling cloak of thick gray wool, picked up his shepherd's crook of stout heart-oak, and stepped into the yard to divide up the herd.

Strong Jack picked the largest sheep, with broad backs and thick thews.

Fast Jack picked the leanest sheep, with quick darting eyes and long legs built for running.

Slow Jack thought about it for most of the day, but finally picked an old black ram and three young ewes. The remainder he split between his two older brothers.

The three brothers clasped hands and bid each other farewell. Each brother chose a different road and set out into the world with their sheep.

Now, as all you fine folk know, the three brothers had many adventures on their journey. Fast Jack and the Fire Dogs. Strong Jack and the Giant's Riddle. Slow Jack and the Final Dance. Taletellers and story-singers throughout the globe all know these, and a thousand thousand children can repeat them all by heart.

But very few know the last story of the Three Brothers Jack. And even fewer of those have the heart to tell it.

The three brothers met at a crossroads, each leading his own flock. Strong Jack had lost a few and Fast Jack had eaten a few, but Slow Jack still had his one old black ram and three young ewes.

The three brothers laughed and clasped hands. Strong Jack and Fast Jack talked all at once, sharing their adventures. A fire was built, a fine stew was cooked, and the brothers were happier than they'd been in many long years and miles.

In the quiet of the night, when the Red Moon shone, Slow Jack finally spoke.

"I've been thinking for a long, long time on the road and this is what I know. The happiest time in my life was when we all lived as one and tended the flocks amongst the green hills. I have searched short and long, near and far, for the perfect place to build our home, and it is very near to this place."

Strong Jack and Fast Jack jumped up in excitement and immediately agreed that this was their brother's best idea.

"Wait a minute," Slow Jack said. "There's a catch."

SPELL/SWORD

The two older brothers sat and listened.

"To get there, we must pass through the Wheelbrake Marsh. Just to the north, past the crossroads. It is an evil place, and the home of a foul and dangerous witch. No roads lead around the swamp, so we have to find a way to get us and our sheep to the other side."

The three brothers sat in silence. They had all heard of the Gray Witch of the Wheelbrake. Many dark songs and broken tales of madness and death.

Strong Jack held out his hand, and Fast Jack was quick to take it. Slow Jack clasped his brothers' hands, and they knew they were in agreement.

The next morning the three brothers found themselves on the edge of the Wheelbrake Marsh. It was gray and green and black and yellow. Dead leaves on stagnant water, bracken and bones, and the sorrow of children who learn that their mother can die.

Fast Jack ran straight in, bounding from tree to tree, his yellow boots shining. His sheep followed, plunging into the stinking waters of the marsh as quick as they could.

His brothers called for him to wait, but Fast Jack didn't listen. He and his sheep disappeared amongst the sawbone trees and sallow water.

Strong Jack sighed and reached out with his mighty arms. One by one, he stacked his sheep on his back until they were all piled high. A tower of bleating white wool, wobbling a bit at the top.

"Let me go ahead brother and make sure it is safe. I will

133

find a dry place in the center, and throw my sheep to the far side. Don't worry, I've done it before and they quite enjoy it." He smiled, and pushed forward into the marsh without waiting for an answer.

Slow Jack watched the sheep tower get lower and lower across the marsh, until the last bleating block disappeared beyond the edge of his vision.

The final brother sat on a broad, gray stone and thought. He thought as the sun crossed the sky, and the moons began to rise.

As last he stood up and set out across the Wheelbrake Marsh, his path lit only by moonlight. The Red Moon was full, the White and Black mere cat's-eye crescents.The old black ram and the three young ewes followed, bleating with fear.

Slow Jack slogged through the stinking water of the swamp, taking great care with each footfall.

He found his brother, Fast Jack, spiked to a tree with daggers of blue glass. His blood ran down the rotting tree bark, and his heart had been neatly ripped from his chest. The sheep were nowhere to be seen.

He found his brother, Strong Jack, neck deep in a pool of yellow mud. Beetles and worms poured from his open mouth and empty eyes. The sheep were nowhere to be seen.

Slow Jack slogged through the stinking water, his heart full of bent steel, his eyes full of cold blood.

At last he came to a dry place in the center of the swamp. A house made of a great mussel shell waited, and a fire was

SPELL/SWORD

burning merrily. An old woman sat next to the fire, turning a spit laden with river fish.

Slow Jack sat down at the witch's fire -- for of course it was she -- and took off his boots. He sat them close to the fire so they could dry. The old black ram and the three young ewes kept their distance, staying on the edge of the island.

"Why?" he said.

"Because the stone rolls down the hill, because the milk spoils, because the button falls off the coat," cackled the Gray Witch of the Wheelbrake, nickel and agate shining in her teeth.

Slow Jack looked into the fire and closed his eyes. He thought and thought. The witch reached across the fire and opened his throat with a fish knife.

No one knows what happened to the sheep.

A moment of quiet, then a shocked intake of breath. The inn erupted in angry shouts and the clamor of chipped mugs being banged on wooden tables. A few rough laughs sounded, and refills were called for.

The flute player ignored the clamor and leaned across the table, poking Rime with her flute.

"That's why no one ever tells this tale," Larabell said. "No one wants to hear the story where the heroes fall."

"And we don't want your story to end the same,"Canteen

added. "So, please, please ... don't go anywhere near Wheelbrake Marsh."

Rime said nothing. She was carefully inscribing every word of Larabell's tale on a clean page in the Book of Hope.

12

The horse slobbered in exhaustion, its sides heaving. Bronberry kicked the dumb beast to keep it moving; the outskirts of Talbot were just coming into sight. Warm orange lights smoldered in the windows, chimney smoke rising. The guard grinned with relief and reviewed the story he would spin for the captain.

"Terrible shame, boss. We made it as far as the canyons, when a mountain lion spooked my horse. You know I'm not much of a rider, so I lost control of the damned nag." The guard kicked his exhausted mount again for emphasis.

He was very proud of that detail. The best lies always made yourself look like a fool. It made people gobble them down all the quicker.

"By the time I got control of my horse, the prisoner got loose, and had gutted that poor, poor girl." Bronberry made his face drop with sadness. A shame he had no mirror to practice with.

"I know you would have liked me to apprehend the

monster, but I was so angry I ran him through before I stopped to think. That poor girl!" he lamented, then tried again, with more emphasis. "That poor, *poor girl*."

"And you won't believe what happened to the wagon! And the other horses..." Bronberry scratched his nose. That part could stand with a little more polish. Was it too outlandish to think that the prisoner boy had somehow killed the horses?

He was passing the side of Enoch's barn, the first building on the edge of town, when he realized what was making his nose itch. He looked up from the contemplation of his lies and the horse's neck and stared.

The chimney smoke was more than a simple hearth fire. Every building in the town was ablaze. In the town square, half-a-hundred villagers stood huddled together, bruises and cuts on many of their faces. A group of men in dark leather stood guard, spears held with military venom.

Around the perimeter of the square purple-black snakes with wings screeched and rustled. They were outfitted with snug saddles made from grass and bone; a few spearmen seemed to be tending to them, keeping them calm. The fire excited the sinuous beasts. Bronberry saw the pea-soup eyes flicker and dart.

It was all behind a pane of glass. Bronberry could feel the heat and smell the smoke, but it was a million miles away. It probably was a bit of a stretch to think the prisoner killed the horses, they ran away in the struggle. The girl's wagon lost. Such a shame, it would have fetched a fair price.

A pair of spearmen pulled him roughly from the saddle and dragged him towards the guard house. A third spearman led his horse away. *Probably to the stables for feed and a rubdown. Lucky old nag.*

Three figures stood in front of the guard house. A tall man wearing armor. A woman with pale yellow hair, cut just below the chin. Bronberry straightened his collar unconciously. And a gray-leather-clad figure, spinning a dagger idly across his knuckles. The orange-skinned creature saluted the blonde guard casually as he approached, tapping his knife against bone-growths like sea coral that sprouted from his brow.

Captain Ruck's lumpy body was spread across the steps. They had been cruel to the old man. Dark bruises covered his face, black blood shimmered. A white sword sprouted from the captain's back like a vicious tree. It was all one piece, smooth metal from blade to hilt. Bronberry watched as an iron gauntlet closed around the alabaster blade and pulled it free with a jerk.

The blade rose, red smear on white. The point came up level with Bronberry's eyes.

"Who is this?" a calm voice said. And the pane of glass broke.

"I will tell you things. Every thing that I have ever known, seen, tasted or touched. Please, please don't kill me, mighty lord." Bronberry found himself kneeling.

The iron-clad knight smiled. His face was thin, hair gray at the temples. A librarian or university scholar.

"That will certainly save us time. Won't it, Ms. Belaine?"

"Mmm," the woman replied, her eyes suddenly filling with yellow light.

The woman moved her hands quickly through several strange gestures, and began to whisper quietly to herself. *Wizard!* Bronberry felt his scalp crawl, as though a thousand ants nested there. Then the sensation was gone.

"This one knows something. He's seen her," Cotton said, light fading. "He'll be telling us shortly."

The white blade hung in the air, then sang as it arced back into the sheath at the iron knight's side.

"Tell us, my friend," he said calmly. "Tell us what you know about the young *doma*, Rime Korvanus."

Jonas snored. Rime's eyes bored a hole into the wooden walls of the inn. The two bards were wrapped in an amorous embrace on the rusty steel bedframe across the room, covers and flesh quaking. The mage stared straight ahead, distant as the three moons of Aufero.

"The button falls off the coat," she whispered.

13

Jonas had the worst hangover. All hangovers are the worst when they're yours.

He lay face-down on the floor, nose bent painfully against the cedar planks. A thin trickle of lava seemed to have spouted somewhere east of his left ear. His eyes were on backwards, and a pair of hedgehogs were rolling around behind his forehead.

And his right arm was asleep. The squire made himself roll over on his back and rubbed his dead arm gingerly. His eyes fell on a clay ewer perched on a small table. He reached out, stretching for the pitcher, praying it was full to the brim with cool water. But it was just out of reach. He would have to actually get up if he wanted the water.

Life is full of small heroics.

He had just laid quivering hands on the ewer, when Rime entered the room and slammed the door behind her. Jonas yelped and dropped the ewer into his lap, where it promptly sloshed the paltry cupful it held onto his trousers.

Life is full of small tragedies.

"Get up," Rime said. "I have provisions and ample direction. Let us be on our way."

"I don't wanna." Jonas flopped back onto the floor, and pulled the cloak over his head. He noted that he was not wearing a shirt. *Need to find that.*

The mage kicked the squire squarely in the side.

"Ow! Why are you kicking me? Stop, stop it!"

"Get up. Get up." Rime's kicks were metronome-steady.

Jonas flared up from the floor in a quick spasm, grabbing the mage's shoulders and lifting her off the ground. Rime continued to kick and tried to wriggle free.

"Good. You're up. Let's go," she said.

"Listen here, little girl. My head hurts. A lot. I don't need you coming in here kicking me in the side. I don't know where we're going, or why you're in such a hurry, or how we're going to get there with no food or water, or any supplies--"

"I have supplies."

"You have supplies? Where did you get supplies? Why didn't you tell me?" Jonas lowered the mage back to her feet. She was very short. The top of her head barely came to his breastbone.

142

"I did. Idiot. That's what 'provisions' means." The mage brushed his hands away and took a step back.

"I know that. I just misheard you," The squire pulled his cloak down to cover his chest and started hunting for his shirt.

"Right. I traded that lump of *olistone* we found to the blacksmith for bread, half a wheel of cheese, and some goat jerky. He also threw in two large waterskins and a satchel because I reminded him of his daughter." Rime flipped the bag off her shoulder as she recounted its contents.

"Traded the... wha? That brown rock?"

Rime threw the satchel into the squire's arms. Hard.

"Glafaghl." Jonas wobbled and fell on his ass, clutching at the satchel.

The mage turned and walked out of the room.

Jonas struggled to his feet. "Hey, Rime! ... wait!"

He quickly scooped up his sweat-soaked shirt and pulled his head and one arm through. He was still wearing his boots, so no worries there. The satchel spun over his shoulder with ease, but then a wave of nausea forced him to lean against the wall for a moment.

Then another moment.

Jonas tapped his forehead firmly against the wood, the fresh pain aligning his brain into something approaching coherence. He pulled himself around the doorway and started flopping down the stairs.

143

He reached the front door of the inn, his stomach turning as the smell of fresh fish stew hit his nostrils. The squire leaned against the doorframe to steady himself, then he remembered.

Sheepishly, he lumbered back into the room and retrieved his sword from the corner.

It was already early afternoon when Jonas emerged, blinking. Rime turned and stepped out into the street.

The mage's thoughts fell like steel marbles onto a cheap ceramic plate. The squire was an idiot who couldn't keep a memory in his head past a few tankards. Cracks formed on the plate. If she had better resources, she would enlist another guard. *Even those two flighty bards would be better.* And he smelled terrible... sour milk poured over wet cedar. The ceramic plate shattered, and her steel thoughts thudded into the dense earth below.

"Where... uh - hey, where are those ladies we met?" he was quick to follow. "Can... Can... Can...?"

"Canteen. And Larabell. I rose at dawn, and they were still asleep. I returned and they were gone. They are of no concern to us."

"But they were so nice. And didn't they give us some, advice... or something?"

Rime stepped over a pile of fish guts in the street without breaking stride. "Their tale was... informative. But I'm sure the folk tradition of storytelling has grossly exaggerated

SPELL/SWORD

and obscured the true nature of the Wheelbrake and... any of its occupants."

Jonas shook his head, and ran both hands through his thick hair. He let out a guttural cry, trying to clear his thicker head. "Gruh. But wait, are you saying that we're going there? Isn't there a witch? That's what you're saying, right?"

"No witch, at least not in the commonly held conception of a tawdry hag. There is a woman in the Wheelbrake Marsh of immense knowledge and power. I need her assistance."

The two travellers were crossing back over the broad, white expanse of the immaculate roadway, and Rime turned sharply to the right, intending to cross the river. The bridge seemed to float effortlessly across the brown river. White arcs rose at the center, with thin cylindrical poles evenly spaced. The mage laid a delicate hand on a beam. It was barely a finger-width, yet held the weight of many tons of stone.

Jonas sweated and cursed, the afternoon sun uncomfortably warm. "Why? What do you need to see this woman for, especially in such a hurry?"

The girl said nothing and continued across the bridge.

"Okay. That's it... stop. Dammit, Rime - stop!" His hand closed around her elbow and pulled the mage around to face him. The mage wrinkled her nose and stared unblinking at the squire.

"Tell me... just tell me what is going on." Jonas was shaking, Rime guessed more from his hangover then any true emotional distress. "You need to see this witch -- or whatever she is. And since I met you -- two, three days ago? All you've done is rush. You're not the sort to do this on a flight of fancy, and it's clear you're not heading towards a box social. So, what? What is it that's driving you? And what's waiting for us?"

"A box social. What in the world is a box social?"

"It's a ...uh...a party where the ladies prepare a boxed lunch, and then the gentlemen each select one of the boxes and then dance with the matching girl." Jonas said, taken aback. "It's fun."

"It sounds like it."

The girl sighed. The two of them stood a third of the way across the white bridge, several of the fisherfolk of Jericho passing by saw the two and winked and nudged each other knowingly. The two looked for all the world like a pair of young lovers, the boy being adroitly put in his place by the delicate young girl.

Jonas realized he had been holding onto her elbow with a firm grip for the entirety of his grand speech and let go awkwardly. The girl hadn't reacted or cried out at all, and he knew his strength was considerable.

"Just tell me," he said.

"Why? My life is one of necessity. You were hired to carry a sword and fight those that I cannot. That is the end of your function, the total of your purpose. A sword doesn't need to know why it is swinging through the air or whose blood flows. You don't need to know anything about me, or where we're going, so I have no reason to tell you."

Jonas shifted his feet and set his jaw. "Tell me, or I'm not

146

SPELL/SWORD

going another step."

Rime's eyes widened in surprise, then flared with anger.

"Then stay here. I don't care." The mage reached up and wrenched the satchel off of the squire's shoulder.

Jonas grabbed one part of the handle. "Don't do this. Rime, this is a bad idea. Don't."

"Let go of my satchel," she hissed. "Go back to the inn and stick your head in a winepot. Maybe there's some locals you can fight, and end up right back in a cell where I found you."

"That's not fair, Rime. Look, I'm sorry, but I'm not letting go. I'm not letting you go off by yourself." His hand tightened on the scarred leather of the strap.

The anger in Rime's eye turned purple. Then the purple began to burn. A thin bolt of it crackled across, detonating in Jonas' chest. The squire toppled backwards and landed on his ass for the second time since waking up.

He batted at his chest dumbly, trying to put out the flames-- but found none. No singes or burns; Rime's magic had been pure force. She backed away, eyes on fire , teeth clenched. Jonas got up, his hand tight on the strap of his sword case.

"Real mature, Rime! That's... that's fine! I'll just stay here -- I know how to fish, I'll fit right in! Do you hear me, Rime? Ms. Rime..whatever your last name is! I'll bet you don't make it a mile before you come running... Rime!"

Jonas started running, and she immediately saw the reason. Dark wings had crested the edge of the horizon to the

147

west, and eight or nine sleek serpentine forms were making a beeline for the city. It had been a long time since she'd seen wyverns, -- and these were battle-dressed, with competent-looking riders wearing dark leather. A cluster of screams began to rise from the village of Jericho.

A pair of wyverns broke off from the main group and made a swift sweep to the south, coming up the river towards the bridge.

Purple wings -- white bridge -- brown water; Jonas felt like he could see everything. Rime had stopped, looking at the approaching creatures with narrow eyes. The squire laid a hand on her shoulder and kept his sword in a defensive position.

"Friends of yours?"

Rime pushed his hand away.

The first wyvern soared past the bridge and circled around -- but the second managed to land on top of the smooth white arc, snake tail winding around the tiny white supports. A figure atop craned his head left and right.

"Put your sword up. Do you see anyone else in this town who has one?" the mage hissed, smacking the squire's shoulder.

Too late. The wyvern-rider pointed triumphantly towards the two travelers and leaped from the saddle. A thin rope uncoiled from his side, allowing him to land safely on the bridge.

Jonas blinked in confusion. The figure was dressed in gray

148

leather armor, and squat mushroom-shaped bones seemed to be growing out of his brow.

"Devil-kin," Rime said, and the squire recognized the orange-toned skin peeking between the creature's handwraps and above the high collar of his armor. The devil-kin held one hand up in a calming gesture, while the other crept towards the two hilts slung over his shoulder.

"Hey now, kid. Doesn't have to go down like this. We need to talk to the girl, best step aside." The creature's voice was friendly gravel, but Jonas kept his eyes on the orange hand and the two sword hilts.

"That's not going to happen," the squire said and attacked, right in the middle of his sentence. A cheap trick, but one that had saved his life a time or two.

Jonas made a broad slash, directly across the center of his foe's body. The squire blinked, and two swords blocked his own. One red, one gray. The devil-kin held the two swords loosely with one hand, his fingers twined around the two thin hilts. Jonas grunted. It was like pushing his blade against a stone wall.

"Aww. Was that fast? That seemed like it was fast," the gray-leather fighter said. "Do you want to try again?"

I didn't even see him move. I didn't even see him move. I didn't even see him move.

Jonas took a step back, then quickly lunged. A simple feint. The devil-kin parried it lazily and spun, intercepting the squire's overhand slash that followed. He still held the two sword hilts in one hand, like an innkeeper with beer bottles.

"You've got some skill, kid... or someone drilled you to death is more likely." The devil-kin yawned. "Look, you're not on my list. How about you just sit this one out?"

The squire's hand was sweaty. He looked up at the wyvern and through the thin white columns out across the river. He locked eyes with the devil-kin and moved to attack again.

"You... you're not super bright, are you?" The devil-kin sighed. He tossed the red sword into his free hand, and tucked the gray blade back over his shoulder. "Sunhammer!"

The red sword erupted into flames, and Jonas' good steel sizzled as it met the other. *A magic sword!*

The squire really hoped that Rime had a plan.

Rime had a plan.

The squire was clearly outmatched, the flaming sword moving at the speed of sarcasm. The devil-kin's eyes were flat and bored. Jonas moved desperately from attack to defense, his feet shifting constantly. The mage calculated that her bodyguard could delay the attacker for no more than fifteen seconds.

Her mind drew a sand-glass next to the devil-kin, the grains falling slowly as her thoughts accelerated. Next she drew a line plotting the arc of the second flying beast. It would cross the bridge in five seconds, but the pilot seemed to be having some difficulty with the reins. It was unlikely that the pilot could land the wyvern as precisely as the devil-kin. Low priority.

The fishermen of Jericho were fleeing the bridge and moving to protect their homes. Rime splashed gray paint on them. They were unimportant for now. Two wyverns here on the bridge, four on the far edge of the town, and three that seemed to be moving in the direction of the bridge.

The plan was simple: disable the devil-kin and his magic sword, then escape. The amount of magic it would take to kill him would leave her totally defenseless against the other pursuers.

Another mind-drawn grain of sand fell: time to act. Rime ran her eyes along the immaculate white columns of the bridge. Precursor construction always comforted her. Each measurement was exact, all arcs and angles completely balanced. No errors in the calculations, numbers and lines danced up the bridge's supports, reassuring to her mind's eye. She reached down into her magic and raised her left hand, pointing toward the left side of the bridge.

A short burst of white flame, then she immediately moved her arm and fired off a burst of blue flame at the supports on the right side. Rime waited exactly two seconds and fired a final burst at an acute angle above the heads of Jonas and the devil-kin.

A grain of sand fell.

The bolt of white flame hit the left side and unfurled into a thick mass of white fabric -- knotted ropes, thick and strong. She had modelled them in her mind after the strange walls of Jericho. The blue bolt hit the right side of the bridge, hitting dead center on a support beam and bouncing across the bridge moving diagonally. Another ricochet or two and the devil-kin noticed; parrying the squire's latest attack and looking over at Rime.

"Wha..?" he began, raising his sword high to finish the squire. Then the blue bolt bounced off the final beam and exploded into the devil-kin's left side, blowing him laterally into the thick web of white ropes. They coiled around his ankles and wrists.

The flaming sword, Sunhammer, spun in the air where he had just been standing. Rime's last bullet hit it squarely-flinging it directly upwards into the underbelly of the passing wyvern. The beast screamed in pain and completely missed its attempt to perch on the bridge, falling clumsily towards the brown water.

Jonas spun around in confusion, his eyes wide. "Wow!"

The trapped devil-kin laughed, spitting a gibbet of blood down his collar. "Okay. That was pretty cool."

Rime wavered slightly but then pulled her chin up. "Let's go."

The squire trotted over, but began looking worriedly over his shoulder. "But the people... and those nice bard-ladies..."

"These people are chasing me. If we leave, they will follow."

"Are you sure, Rime?"

"Yes, I'm sure! Now let's go."

The devil-kin cleared his throat. Once he had their attention, he jerked his head toward the town-end of the

152

bridge.

A ball of light soared over the town, and landed at the end of the bridge. It faded, revealing a trim blonde woman, and a gray-haired knight. The woman's eyes still shimmered with her spell. Rime marked her as the primary target, her mind drawing arcs and trajectories, plotting her avenues of attack.

Then her eyes slid over to the old knight and saw the emblem on his breastplate.

A white spiral, coiled into a teardrop.

The lines and numbers and arcs and calculations evaporated. Rime stared into a blank universe and shook with fear.

The knight walked slowly forward across the bridge, the blonde wizard a half-step behind.

"Doma Rime Korvanus, please don't make this more unpleasant than it has to be." His voice was steady and plain, almost comforting. "You are a danger. To yourself and everyone you encounter. The Magic Wild is forbidden for a reason, a brushfire in the summer forest. Come, child, let me take you home."

Jonas raised his sword half-heartedly and stepped forward to defend. Rime grabbed his free hand and knit her fingers with his. The squire was as shocked by the gesture, as he was by the strength of her grip.

"Don't. Let. Go," she said through clenched teeth, and her eyes flared a brilliant red.

The old knight calmly laid a gauntlet on the pommel of his

sword.

Rime jerked the squire up into the air as her red energy propelled them skyward. Jonas managed to get his sword back into its scabbard and hung on.

Rime was terrified. She reached down deep, deeper than she was normally comfortable, and felt the embers of her magic ignite. She gathered her fear and rage into an orb of flame, large as her hand, large as a wagon-wheel, large as a house, and flung it down on the calm-faced knight.

Her vision went black, but she kept the magic in her grip. Her flight carried them both to the saddle of the devil-kin's wyvern. She grimly wrapped Jonas' hands in the reins as the purple beast screeched. Her mind reached out and filled the beast with fear, with endless terror. It must fly, fly faster than it ever had, or die a most terrible death.

The wyvern flung itself into the air, its wings beating feverishly. Jonas felt the mage's weight collapse onto his hand as her magic faded. He held onto her and desperately tried to pull both of them into the saddle. They dangled half-off the terrified creature and found themselves looking down at the white bridge.

Jonas and Rime saw the fire of her magic suspended in the air, a handspan from the old knight. He held aloft a long white sword, slender and unbroken from tip to pommel.

The ball of fire imploded, absorbed by the white blade, sucked in like a hungry whirlpool. The blond wizard was kneeling in pain a few paces behind the knight.

Rime cried out and tried to reach for more of her magic, but it slipped from her fingers and her mind went dark.

SPELL/SWORD

Purple wings beat the air, and Jonas did his best to not let go.

"I am sorry, Cotton. I did not have time to warn you," Linus said, helping her to her feet.

Cotton wiped her mouth with the back of her hand and nodded. The white sword was anathema to any sort of magical energy, and wizards often found being close to it extremely uncomfortable. When it had absorbed the wild mage's fire, the pain between her temples was hot and sharp.

They walked together across the white bridge to where the devil-kin Sideways hung.

"Well, that didn't go too well," he said. "Help a fellow down?"

"Her power is great, Linus." Cotton ignored his plea. "Stronger than Barl the Sky-Burner, I'd say."

"Perhaps," the knight replied and reached again for his weapon. "Stand back please, Ms. Belaine."

The wizard took several steps back, as he brandished the white sword. The ropes holding the assassin were absorbed into the blade, and he landed primly on his toes.

"The wyvern is panicked, it'll fly plenty fast, but I don't peg either of them as trained riders. The rest of the wing can easily follow. Most likely we're going to find them with their heads cracked on a lonely mountainside somewhere. Or in the beast's belly." Sideways turned, and peered through the white beams. "Speaking of, better go retrieve my weapon. Then we can go right after them."

"On a Hunt, the most important weapon is knowledge. We have learned a great deal about our quarry in this encounter. Powerful, smart, adaptable. She surveyed the situation dispassionately and made excellent decisions given her limited options and resources. Knowledge gained in Talbot was minimal, even with that guard's help. They were most likely here for at least a day. Let us see what knowledge we can glean from the fine fisher folk of Jericho," Linus said.

"You sound as if you admire her," Cotton said with revulsion. "A filthy wild mage, an abomination."

"You must love your prey, Ms. Belaine." The old knight turned and headed back towards the town. "Know them better than they know themselves. Only then can you strike, and be sure your aim is true."

14

The leather reins cut into Jonas' hand, and he yelped as the wyvern lurched higher into the sky. Rime's unconscious body dangled from his other hand, knuckles white around her tiny wrist. His shoulder ached, but the mage's form was light enough to allow him to keep his grip. The purple scales of the beast were fetid with some yellow growths, and a slick sheen of sweat slid liberally out from under the saddle.

I woke up thirty minutes ago with a hangover.

The scrub pine and rocky slopes of the earth below spun beneath his feet. His two worn boots got an excellent view of the mountains below, rising up from the river flatlands, steep hills dotted with thick evergreens and oaks with golden leaves.

Jonas looked up at the saddle and saw that the seat made a rough bucket with high sides. He hoped it was large enough for two riders at a time. A large brass ring hung off the side, and he automatically reached for it with his left hand, then remembered he was holding onto Rime.

The wyvern banked to the right, and Jonas swung once more over empty air. His stomach turned outside-in.

Never...drinking...again...

The wyvern leveled off and put on another burst of speed.

Okay, got to do something quick -- before I lose my grip, or this damned beast breaks my arm.

Uttering a thick groan, Jonas pulled on the reins with his right hand. He was fortunate; the reins were looped around the saddle's horn, so the wyvern didn't turn again. His arm bent slowly, pulling his body up the side of the beast by vicious, painful inches.

At last his head reached level with the lip of the saddle. The thick scent of leather barely covered the mottled stench of the purple scales beneath. Without stopping or allowing himself to think, he pulled hard with his other arm. The tension in his shoulders and chest was excruciating, but the mage's body rose until her arm was level with his chest. *Gotta...gotta...gotta...push...*he was panting, his face crushed with exertion. The squire's right shoulder exploded with pain as he shifted his weight onto it and pushed the mage up higher.

Jonas panicked. If she was awake, she could easily grab the lip of the saddle, but he couldn't get her high enough like this, to get her weight over the top.

"Urrrr..." he said, through clenched teeth.

I have to switch my grip somehow. I have to... An idea clicked into place, and he pulled her over to his right arm, pinning her body between him and the wyvern's flank. Rime's face flopped against his neck, and he let go of her wrist. He stretched his fingers for a second, and grabbed the mage's bottom. Her head lolled back, and Jonas thought he saw her eyes flicker open for a brief, terrifying moment. It was just a trick of the light, but he composed a quick prayer.

Please -- just don't have her wake up while I'm holding onto her ass. This predicament, the devil-spawn with the flaming sword, and this hangover are quite enough.

Jonas fished around until he got a good grip on the waist of her leggings and heaved. Pushing with his free arm and as much weight as he could add with his chest and head, he managed to get the front half of her over the lip of the saddle. One last shove, and she tumbled face forward into the wide leather bucket.

The squire weakly grabbed the brass ring with his free hand, and allowed his right arm to relax for a moment. He panted against the side of the saddle, and briefly considered just hanging there for a while. The wyvern's screech brought him to his senses. One last surge and he pulled himself up into the saddle next to the unconscious mage.

His head spun, and he gave himself a few precious moments to catch his breath and rub blood back into his aching shoulders and hands. His right hand was torn and blistered from the reins. He slowly unwound them and held them loosely in his teeth while he inspected the damage. Nothing permanent, just painful.

Jonas took the reins in both hands and got up on his knees. He rolled Rime over on her back; she fit quite snugly in the back portion of the saddle. The squire peered behind them. There was no sight of the river, the city of Jericho, or any pursuit. He turned and faced forward, over the sinuous neck and head of the wyvern.

A blast of wind hit him, and Jonas saw the sky for the first time. He'd looked at it many times in his life, watching storm clouds for rain or trying to guess the time by the sun's position. But this time he didn't just look at it, he saw it. It was blue, but not really. The edge of the horizon hung over the mountains and darkened almost to purple; as his eyes moved upwards the blue got lighter and lighter until it was almost white where it touched the sun. The clouds were worlds of their own, white and ash twisted like old gnarled roots and stretched like feather-cotton across the bowl of the heavens.

The ground flowed underneath the wyvern's wings. The creature seemed to be slowing, its terror beginning to wane. The wind caught his brown cloak, the thin fabric popped and flowed behind him.

The squire found himself grinning. If he was a poet he would have wept, but his square-shaped soul did not have that reaction to offer. The pure wonder of the moment hit him, then bent around the blunt corners of his imagination and spun away. But he would never forget this moment.

He felt like the whole world was his.

Jonas looked down at the reins in his hands, running to a metal bit in the wyvern's mouth.

Can't be that different from a horse… can it? He tugged on the left rein.

Rime woke up, her head slumped over the squire's neck. Her hands were knotted across his chest, and Jonas held her legs loosely. She was hanging from his back like a sack of grain.

The squire was sweating and hiking down a hillside dotted with spare green cedars.

SPELL/SWORD

"Bluh-- where... what's going on?" she demanded.

"You're awake!" Jonas said cheerfully without slowing pace.

The mage took a deep breath, then immediately regretted it. Her bodyguard smelled like a rotting barn full of steamed cabbage. He was unpleasantly warm, and sweat dripped from his curly hair directly down her collar. Better than what she had faced on the white bridge, but only slightly.

"Stop. Stop trotting and put me down."

"I don't know, Rime. You've been out all night and most of the day. I tried to get some water in you, but it just dribbled down your chin." Fresh drops of sweat swung across her forehead.

Very only slightly.

It had been early morning when they departed Jericho; Rime looked up at the sun. It was nearing the horizon. It would be dusk soon. She had been unconscious for nearly a whole day. She suddenly felt cold, and Jonas' stinking heat didn't disturb her as much as it had. She had come very close to dying. Worse than that she had completely lost control. *Without this sweaty fool and that wyvern...*

Rime blinked. Clearly her mind was still half-asleep. "What happened to the wyvern?"

She felt the squire swallow and his shoulders twist.

"Umm... could we just... not talk about that?" Jonas said.

161

"Not talk about that?"

"Yeah, just... not talk about it?"

The mage felt her stomach tighten, and a grin begin to form on her face. She kept her tone severe. "Okay. Not talking about the wyvern. And what happened to it. Just closing the book on that. Completely."

"Thank you," Jonas said.

"Now stop sweating on me and put me down."

The squire grunted and came to a halt. He moved over near a large granite outcropping and leaned his back against it. Rime took her hands apart and found them bound. Jonas ducked under her hands and hurriedly untied them.

"I'm sorry about the rope, Rime, but I had to make sure you wouldn't fall off."

Rime was impressed. An actual good idea planned and executed. She rubbed the blood back into her legs and peered around the hillside. They were above a long narrow valley; she could just glimpse a thin blue stream winding its way northwards. Another good idea: he had been following the stream but had kept far enough away to avoid any pursuit following the water's track with plenty of natural cover. All while she hung lifeless as a sack of potatoes on his back.

"As best I can tell the wyvern carried us due east from Jericho, so once we... uh... landed, I headed north. I remembered that the swamp where you wanted to go was north-west of the town, so I figured I'd head north for a

SPELL/SWORD

while, then we could swing back west once we were clear of whoever those guys were."

"It's fine," she said and pushed herself off the rock.

Her legs crumpled, nerveless. She slid a few feet down the hill before Jonas caught her.

"Whoa -- you all right?"

"Don't touch me. Leave me alone." Rime said, face down in the dirt.

The squire tried desperately to fight back a rogue chuckle. "Rime, I can't leave you alone or you'll slide a few dozen more feet into that briar thicket."

"That's not a briar thicket, it's a species of nettle called *jillfang*. Common herbalists call it Ghost Pricker Bush, due to its odd white coloration before it blooms. Useful in a tea to prevent arthritis and cataracts." Rime splayed her fingers, digging into the coarse soil.

Jonas sighed and picked her up. He carted her back over to the outcropping and sat her back upright. Then, displaying remarkable wisdom, he walked away several paces.

"You need to eat. The bread got pretty squashed but it tastes alright. I'll slice you some cheese, and you should try to get down some jerky as well," the squire said, businesslike.

Rime looked down at her hands and the small stones and dirt crammed under her nails. She hated the squire, hated him for seeing her like this, hated him carrying her this far, hated him for keeping her alive. Hated that soon he would

163

need to pick her up again and carry her still farther.

Jonas brought over the food, and she took it and put it in her mouth. The squire grunted in satisfaction and passed her the waterskin. He chewed on a slender slice of cheese and looked down the hillside with the mage.

Rime felt sick for the first few bites, but her stomach was eager. She felt her vision sharpen, and a few numbers emerged -- cautious and barely gleaming. The river was 540 feet away, the average height of the trees within her range of vision was 6.2 feet.

"I told you before that I was a wild mage. Do you really know what that means?" she began.

"That you're like a regular wizard, just more... wild? Kind of like strawberries that grow in the garden, and the kind you find out in the woods."

"I... what? A strawberry? That's the best you have? A strawberry?" A few sixes and sevens floated over the squire's head, doing various impressions of his guilty look. "Hundreds of years of arcane history, entire nations nearly toppled and burned by wild mages and you think I'm some sort of market produce?"

"I'm sorry! You said it like I should know what it was, and the guard-guy did the same, so I just kind of nodded." A fat green eight slapped its forehead.

"Okay. I wanted to explain a few things, but now that I realize that I'm dealing with an infant..."

"Come on, Rime!" The squire's brow was furrowed, and a red flush was starting up the side of his neck. The mage pointed north.

SPELL/SWORD

"Pick me up. We can still make a few more miles before the sun sets. I'll try to cover the gaps in your education."

Just like teacher said. You have to accept the facts. You have to work with the data you have, the resources available. Rime wrinkled her nose as Jonas ducked under her arm.

"Tie my hands again. I don't have the strength to hold on, especially if I fall unconscious." *No point in hating the facts, Rime. Use them or give up.*

Jonas fumbled for a moment, but tied her hands securely.

"Now walk. And listen."

The day was warm, and the regular sway of the squire's gait made Rime drowsy. She allowed her eyes to wander, calculating the circumference of mountain flowers, the radii of tree trunks, and the wing rate of passing bees. Her voice was smooth and level, dispensing information.

"Magic is a useless term. A giant bucket for a swarm of concepts, almost as vague and foggy as 'Energy' or 'Force' or 'Family' or 'Soup'. Throughout the ages it has appeared in different forms. Different methods, different effects. But one thing has remained constant: control. Order. With wands, with spells, with prayers, with dances in the moonlight, with masks, with words, with song." Jonas made a short hop into a ravine and continued north, listening.

"My teacher always said that the energy needs a shape to fill, like water in a cup. If we went to that stream down there and tried to pull water out with our bare hands, it would be futile. But a cup, a bucket, a dam -- even a ditch dug in the earth can channel the water."

"Your teacher sounds nice," the squire interrupted.

"He beat me with a cane until I bled through my shirt. Now, shut up." Rime's tone did not change. "The Wizard College in Valeria is the group that most people are familiar with; that blonde woman we saw on the bridge, she was clearly a wizard. They have many different methods of using this natural energy -- lots of different cups. Different sizes, different shapes. But once in a while, someone is born who doesn't need a cup. The water flows where they want it to, *because* they want it to. They ignore all of the rules that the shamans and wizards made, because, for them, there are no rules. Pure energy, wild magic. Wild mage. That's what I am."

Jonas was walking near a tall yellow cedar. The top of his head brushed a low branch, and golden needles sprinkled down on the two travellers. Rime pushed them out of her eyes using the squire's shoulder.

"Some believe that these people are evil, an abomination against the natural order. And many wild mages have gone out of their way to prove this belief. Sweet Jill Barrow, Margus Moonbreaker, Dralith the Night-blood, Jayson Acorn. You know these names, don't you?"

"Uhhhh."

"Of course not," Rime sighed. "They burned cities, uprooted mountains; thousands died screaming in the night. The path of the wild mage is madness and death. Every single one of them fell, the Magic Wild was too much for the mortal mind to contain. And so..."

166

SPELL/SWORD

Jonas stumbled over a root, his knees burned with the strain of catching his balance. Rime did not speak for several paces afterwards.

"...and so the Council of Nine made a decision. Something must be done to protect the world and protect the reputation of true wizards. They formed a legion of mage-killers. Made from the fiercest warriors, the most cunning assassins. Valeria itself supplied mighty wizards trained in fire and battle. They called themselves The Hunt; their sigil is a white spiral shaped like a teardrop.

"The Hunt was very successful. They tracked down and killed every wild mage who showed their heads. Thousands of lives were saved as the maddened abominations were cornered and executed. Bard's Gate was freed from the gift of the Truthspinner, Gorah's children were saved from the perverted rituals of Mika Freeborn. There are even reports of fierce battles with wild shaman on the Northern spires of Marankur. Which is interesting, as the first peaceful contact with some of the fiercer tribes occurred a few short years later by an expeditionary force of Seto pilgrims--"

Jonas cleared his throat. Rime realized she had been dozing off; she gave her head a swift shake, and got back on topic.

"Yes. So. The Hunt killed all the wild mages at large, and then they killed all of the wild mages in hiding. Then they killed all of the wild mages' families, children and infants, just in case the affliction was hereditary. Then they killed anyone who was even suspected -- fortune tellers, healer women, stage magicians. Then they killed their children. The Hunt had become so well connected and powerful that none could easily oppose them. They were single-

167

minded, clever, ruthless, and extremely well hidden. And, to the surprise of no one, this slaughter lead to a massive swell of enrollment in the wizard colleges of Valeria. Any child with even a hint of magical ability was stuffed in a school as quickly as possible, to prevent any chance of precautionary murder by the Hunt. Only wizards, true Valerian wizards trained in their elite academies could safely practice magic. The coffers of Valeria grew fat with gold, and the Council of Nine smiled and congratulated themselves on being staunch defenders of the poor, innocent people throughout the world."

"Rime, you're choking me!" The squire tugged down on her bound hands, freeing his wind pipe.

"They killed a few monsters, made a vast profit, and secured their position as the ultimate authority on magic. Who cares that hundreds of innocents were killed in the process?"

The pair came to a halt under another tall cedar. The sun was approaching the edge of the valley. Long shadows stretched. "We should stop here for the night. It's a good, high place where we can keep an eye out for anyone following us," Jonas said, swinging the mage around to face him and placing her gently on the ground.

"They were disbanded twenty years ago by the Grand Wizard himself. I suppose they never truly vanished." The girl forced her exhausted hands to untie the knots holding her hands together. "That man..."

"Was one of the Hunt, right? The old man with the white sword. What happened, back there on the bridge? I've never even heard of anything like that. The way it just sucked up your magic."

168

SPELL/SWORD

"Ugh. Stop that."

"Stop what?"

"That awful slurping noise you just made."

"Wha..?" Jonas repeated the noise. "It's the sound it made, the sound of your magic being slurped right up."

Rime leaned back against the tree trunk and shut her eyes. She might have been smiling.

The wind blew across the evening hillside. Yellow needles fell. The girl looked through slit eyes and pushed the squire to the side with her boot. "Get out of the way and let me enjoy the sunset."

The squire grunted and sat down on the bed of pine needles. He pulled the satchel off his aching shoulders and bundled his cloak into a makeshift pillow. Jonas laid back and tried to ignore the soreness in his back and legs. The mage was light as a child, but he was beginning to feel the strain of carrying her.

Without really expecting a response, he asked, "Why are we really going to the Marsh?"

"I told you. To see a witch." Rime brushed pine needles out of her hair and went to sleep.

THE HUNT

"To see a witch?" Cotton asked delicately. "You expect me to believe that?"

The wizard spoke quiet words, and the glass rod she held flared with blood-orange light. With a precise touch she sat it against the left cheek of her prisoner. Flesh sizzled and smoked, and the prisoner screamed again. Cotton grabbed the prisoner's head firmly and pushed the burning rod through the skin of her cheek. The prisoner's mouth opened in pain, a band of fire appearing between the teeth. Cotton kept a careful grip on the glass rod and kept pushing until the tip came out the opposite cheek. A horse's bit of orange fire and pain blazed in the prisoner's ruined jaws.

The wizard pushed a strand of blond hair out of her eyes and kept her spell engaged for a ten-count. On eleven, the glass rod went dark.

The prisoner whimpered. Her teeth were black from the heat -- her lips and gums cracked and bleeding. A slow trickle ran down both cheeks, tears mixed with blood.

"Tell me again, talespinner. Can you tell it again?" The blond wizard leaned in close, and whispered in the prisoner's ear. "Can you sing it this time? Can you?"

Linus cleared his throat. "Doma Belaine."

SPELL/SWORD

Cotton's lips twisted. "You'll sing later, I promise you," she whispered, before turning to the knight.

"Her story is unchanged. Her thoughts return again and again to a tale she told in the inn's common room." The glass rod slid smoothly from the prisoner's cheeks, and Cotton wiped it clean with a white cloth. "The same as the fat redhead from this morning."

"Yes, you were very thorough."

Is he judging me? He should know better than that. The wizard caressed a flat green stone laying on the board above the sobbing prisoner's head. "A thoughtstone requires strong mental activity to give the best readings. Pain tends to intensify and clarify a subject's thoughts." She slipped the green stone into a leather pouch. "And we are in a hurry. They are heading towards the Wheelbrake, chasing an old story."

"Interesting. Let us be on our way, then." Linus stood and gestured towards the door, his eyes tired.

Cotton held her right palm over the prisoner's mouth, and spoke a quiet word. Clean, white sand filled the cavity, mingling with the blood. The woman thrashed and choked, and then lay still. The knight raised a reproachful eyebrow, then pushed open the door. The wizard tucked her tools into their pouch at her side and swept past. *I got the job done, old man. Isn't this the 'skill' that you required of me?*

The wizard pushed open the door, trying to control her anger. The knight always had this effect on her. He used her adeptly, a perfect tool for this purpose. But he always looked at her with a quiet reproach. Linus knew about her lover, knew how her lover had used the wild magic to

171

control her, own her, reduce her. The knight's white sword had freed her. Her lover's cruel, mad face going slack above her. She became a second weapon for the Hunter that day. Cotton grew weary of the knight treating her as if she made his hands dirty. She had not spilled a tenth the blood that the white sword had.

The devil-kin was napping in the sun, his head resting on the edge of the low porch. His eyes popped open the moment Cotton's boots hit the wooden deck, and he rolled up onto his feet. He bowed, flipping his arm up in a grandiose manner. The wizard rolled her eyes and walked past him.

The people of Jericho had been easy to cow, as the people of Talbot before them. They all waited meekly in their homes, peeking through brown-tinted windows. A few object lessons in public dismemberment and the fisher folk had been eager to point out anyone that had spoken to the strangers. The blacksmith had been as hard as his anvil, never speaking a word even as Cotton poured more and more pain into him. She had allowed him to live, a mark of respect. The two bards had been much more forthcoming.

Pathetic, weak things. They should have told us what we needed to know immediately. A wild mage is a danger to all.

She swung up into the wyvern's saddle as the beast screeched in annoyance. Sideways slid in behind her, taking great care to avoid touching her. "Linus should have made you walk."

"I didn't see you doing very much against that snip of a girl. Maybe next time I'll pull your beans out of the fire." the devilkin retorted. "And that was the bad wyvern. Bumpy wing-rhythm, it was past its prime, smelled like spoiled bread dough. Doing everyone a favor, them tearing

SPELL/SWORD

off with it."

"Children," the knight said.

The wizard and devil-kin snapped to attention, embarrassed by the reproach. Linus pulled himself into his own saddle and signalled to the rest of their force. The leather-clad mercenaries were renowned in the West for their professionalism, and the flying mounts provided had been a good use of his employer's gold. They were effective fighters but only suitable for delay and diversion tactics. Against the wild mage they would be matches flung into the teeth of a desert whirlwind. He would need to rely on the assassin and wizard -- and his own cunning and experience.

"The Wheelbrake is to the north. A fetid swamp on the coast, thick with bracken and murky salt water. We shall fly to the sea's edge, then move inland, searching for them. Do not engage the wild mage alone; report and regroup so we can bring all of our force to bear. You have witnessed her power..." the knight pointed out across the white bridge of Jericho. The slender columns that had stood for thousands of years, unmarked by time, were broken and melted. Sad candles scorched and marred by the girl's flame. "...take every precaution. A purse of gold to the first man who spots them."

Linus dug his spurs into the wyvern's side, and the beast bellowed. Its wing-mates answered, and The Hunt leaped into the cloudy skies over the city of Jericho.

173

15

"This place stinks," Jonas said.

The tips of his boots hung over sour, green water. Long grasses and cattails sprouted from low hillocks. Every scrap of land and plant was covered with a black slime, shining in the morning light. A low wind blew, smelling of brackish salt and dead crabs. The two travellers stood on the edge of Wheelbrake Marsh, the squire's cloak flapping, and the mage's short hair flung across her face. Rime leaned on a rotting oak branch. She had risen with difficulty at dawn and refused to be carried any farther.

"You stink," Rime replied without any trace of a smile.

The marsh wasn't quite as terrifying as the bard's tale had suggested. An expanse of water, mud, and reeds broken up occasionally by leafless trees. The trunks and branches were gray, shot through with mottled crimson. Dangling from a few were pears - a green pit rolled slowly in golden fluid, sloshing within the translucent skin. Jonas wondered

SPELL/SWORD

what they tasted like, his stomach rumbling.

"Let's go," Rime said. She jabbed her walking stick down into the first pool, testing the depth. She slid in afterwards, the water coming to her navel. The squire groaned quietly and flopped into the pool behind her.

"So, how are we going to find this witch, assuming that she's even real?" He felt dank, green water flowing over the top of his boots. The water was soup-warm.

"The Gray Witch is real. In many legends, a kernel of truth. I have studied every legend, folk tale, nursery rhyme, song, or half-forgotten limerick that mentions her in any way. She is real." Rime pushed through the green water and stumbled over a hidden log.

"I hope so," Jonas said as a dead muskrat floated by.

The two travelers lumbered onto a small bump of land dominated only by a rotting stump. The trunk of the tree extended back down into the water, branches invisible. Jonas put his foot on the trunk and leaned down experimentally. The drowned tree shifted slightly but did not move. A small explosion of bubbles and several dark fish skittered away.

"Fish, hmm," the squire said, his fingers opening and closing. "We could stand with some extra food in the sack."

Rime ignored him and flopped down into the next pool, advancing towards the center of the marsh. She was already showing signs of tiring, her small hands bone-white on her deadwood staff. Jonas sighed and hopped into the green water again after her, but he kept his eyes trained on the water for any swimming meals.

175

The sun rolled across the sky, unconcerned. The two travellers were fortunate that the day was mild. A smooth breeze blew steadily from the coast to the north, beyond their vision where the marsh gave way to unbroken sea. Jonas reslung his blade so that it hung horizontally across his shoulders. The steel would not spend most of the day being dipped in salt water. Rime spoke little, batting the squire's questions out across the endless marsh where they died lonely deaths. She stopped to rest often, leaning against convenient trunks of the pear trees or simply collapsing against the sides of the pools, shoulder propped against the muddy bank. But her eyes stayed locked on the center of the marsh.

Jonas placed his hand under the mage's shoulder and steadied her as she pulled herself up the bank. She didn't resist or remark, so he quickly grabbed her other armpit and hauled her out of the green water. They had been walking for two hours by his best estimation.

"Rime," the squire said carefully. "You need to stop. You're burning yourself up. We have a long way to go, I think."

"I'm fine," she said, clutching her staff. "From the reports I've read, the Marsh is much more dangerous at night. We must find the Witch while the sun shines."

Her face was white with exertion, stretched taut across her fine bones. Jonas realized that she was looking right through him, her eyes distant. Then he looked closer, holding his hand to shade her forehead.

The mage's eyes glowed a faint blue, almost unnoticeable in the direct sunlight but faint candle-wicks of power in the shade.

SPELL/SWORD

"What-- what are you doing? Why are your eyes glowing?"

Rime forced the slump out of her back and stared down the squire. "Not that it's any of your business... it's just a trickle. A slender thread of my magic to keep me moving. It also increases my perception immensely. I can feel something very old and powerful in the center of this marsh, and it can only be the Gray Witch. I'm fine. Don't make me repeat myself again."

She walked past him, keeping her back straight. The mage slid into another pool, and began thrusting her way across.

"But doesn't your magic hurt you or tire you out? How can you use something that tires you out to keep yourself from tiring out?" he said with exasperation, then shouted after her. "That doesn't make any sense."

Rime continued to push forward, almost pulling herself with the staff.

"It doesn't make any sense, Rime." The squire easily caught up with her, splashing across the pool. The mage turned and thumped him across the chest with her staff.

"My magic is my business. Stop wasting time."

"Look, let me carry you again..."he began, but another brisk thump stopped him.

"Reaching the Gray Witch is my goal -- my Quest, if you like. I have risked much and paid much to make it this far, and I will not arrive at her doorstep being carted like a bundle of laundry. Do you understand me?" Her eyes flared a brighter blue, visible even in the sunlight and raised her staff again to strike him.

177

"Fine, fine, you stubborn goat," he said, raising his hands in defeat. "But when you collapse face down in a pile of turtle shit, don't say I didn't warn you."

Jonas slid his hand back under her left shoulder. She bristled, but finally switched the staff to her opposite hand and leaned some of her weight on him.

They traversed three more pools and a slick muddy bank in this manner. They found a long strip of sharp reeds growing from a reasonably solid piece of earth. It extended basically northward towards their destination. Rime was better able to support herself, so the squire set to clearing a path with his sword. He took his time with each swath, doing a very thorough job. It created moments where the mage would have to stop and catch her breath.

"The ground in the Wheelbrake is laced with an acidic strata that causes vegetation and smaller fauna to develop similar adaptations. Almost everything in this marsh is poisonous, especially to the larger sauroids and reptiles. There are no turtles in the Wheelbrake. So, no turtle shit," Rime recited.

The mage sat quietly in the library of her mind and watched her body burn. She closed the book she had been reading, folding the leaves over her hand, one finger still placed on the pertinent passage on turtles.

The books quavered on their neat shelves. The heat and pressure outside was growing, the books squeezed together for comfort and prepared for the worst. The dragons beyond her library coiled around each other, flashes of lightning illuminating their twisted shapes.

SPELL/SWORD

The young girl watched a crack form in the floor, tiny but spreading.

She looked out through the windows of her eyes. The boy was pulling her up a moss-covered log, his face tight. She noticed idly that the matted hair at his temple had curled itself into the High Elven sigil for 'Commerce.'

Then out of the corner of her eye-window, she saw something massive lurch forward out of a flat green pool. Jonas' attention was focused on her, so he didn't see it coming.

Rime sighed and left her library, to do battle.

Of course, it was a turtle. The universe required it to be so.

A vast shell, mottled with reeds and muck, covered in rotting skeletons: alligator, fish, and humanoid. Green water rolled off the black hide as the beast charged forward, fast as a horse could gallop. Rime estimated that it would reach them in fourteen seconds.

She spared a second to finish her survey of the improbable turtle. It was clearly a snapper, its massive jaw already working in anticipation. The edges of its mouth were a flat gray, like unpolished steel. Fierce yellow eyes focused on her and the squire, but they seemed to be having some difficulty focusing on them exactly. *Nocturnal, perhaps? Having difficulty seeing in the late afternoon sun. Interesting.*

The mage tucked her staff close and half leaped into the squire's arms. "Run. Now. Don't ask questions, just run!"

179

Jonas looked surprised but obeyed, picking her up and sliding back down the log into a small pool. He thrashed through the water and onto the bank. Rime watched over his shoulder as the massive snapping turtle tore through the reeds behind them. It skidded to an ungainly stop, its yellow eyes casting around for them like child-lanterns bobbing in the dark.

"Run faster. We need to find cover, a tree... anything to give us an advantage." She craned her neck forward, forcing her mind to survey every line of the marsh ahead. Jonas was momentarily blinded by the flash of blue light from her eyes. He tripped over a root but managed to keep running.

Rime spotted a medium-sized pear tree on a low hill that stood slightly above the rest of the marsh. It wasn't particularly promising, but at least it would give them a solid place to fight out of the water. "There." She pointed, and Jonas headed toward it, beginning to pant.

The mage looked back. The snapping turtle was closing the distance, barely slowing as it hit stretches of water and mud.

The squire threw himself out of the water and up the embankment to the tree. He found a low crook and pushed Rime into it. She dropped her staff in the exchange, grabbing onto the gray branches tightly.

Jonas ripped his sword free, taking it in two hands. He pointed it down the hill where the turtle lumbered forward.A meaty hiss escaped its throat, as it plowed its way out of the water onto their tiny hill. The mage blinked and reached down into her magic, gathering it in her fist.

SPELL/SWORD

Rime's mind was an eagle. She could see it all.

The tree. Her muddy body in the tree. The boy. The sword. The turtle. The hill. The sun behind the tree. Every limb outlined with fire, and the squire's steel was a flat black shadow. The jaws of the turtle opened.

She was tired, so tired. The magic was there as always, but Rime knew. Her body couldn't take much more. She had been leaning on the power all day, for without it she would be a crippled husk, strapped to the squire's back. She could use even more power to destroy this beast, but then she would die.

She would die and never reach her goal.

But she did have enough strength to escape. To fly.

Rime looked at the squire's back, at his hands on the hilt of his sword. She weighed his life like a poker chip.

Necessity.

Without a word, her body ignited with blue flame. The branches of the tree cracked and popped with the heat. Rime burst up into the sky like a comet, arcing towards the center of the marsh and the other power she sensed.

Jonas looked up in alarm, his sword hanging slack in one hand. "Rime... no! Rime!"

She did not look back. She let the magic burn.

16

The squire stood alone on the muddy hill, the pear tree crackling with blue flames. His mouth was wide with shock.

Then the turtle was upon him.

Jonas flung himself to the right, his sword arm impacting with a twisted root. A swift bite of pain as he nicked his left shoulder with the blade. The massive snapping turtle slammed its shoulder into the tree. The squire was only a few feet away, not far enough to avoid the front foot of the turtle, claws like shovel-heads. Jonas rolled desperately away; flat pain raked the back of his legs before he could get back to his feet.

The thick square foot slammed down again into the hillside mud, but Jonas was still moving. Using another root as a foothold, he climbed up into the tree, doing his best to dodge the flames. The blue flames were cold. *Cold*

SPELL/SWORD

flames. Rime, what the hell?

The turtle backed up slightly, then slammed its black head into the lower branches. Steel jaws snapped, and branches and blue flame disappeared into its mouth. A lacework of ice appeared wherever Rime's flame touched the creature, but it paid little mind. Jonas pushed himself further up into the tree, but the branches were too thin to hold his weight. Yellow eyes burned up at him, and the jaws clipped another branch and grimly chopped it down into the beast's gullet.

It's eating its way to me. This thing is going to eat every branch, then me for dessert.

Jonas spun his head around, looking for any chance of escape. The Wheelbrake seethed on for miles in every direction. They'd been lucky to make it this far with the snapping turtle in pursuit. He tightened his grip, one hand on a branch and the other on his sword.

They had been lucky. Now it was just him.

The snapping turtle's head collided with the trunk of the tree and Jonas lost his grip on the branch and tumbled forward. The squire recalled the ogre in Talbot. *Why can't I fight anything my size?*

He landed half on the front of the turtle's shell, his legs dangling off and kicking the side of its massive neck. The squire grabbed the edge of the shell and swung his legs up -- the snapping turtle hissed and raged, its flat head whipping left and right. Jonas swung wild, and his good steel bit into the beast's thick leathery neck.

The turtle roared and charged forward, twisting its bulk against the ravaged pear tree.

183

"Shit!" Jonas said.

The turtle was trying to scrape him off. The squire pulled himself up the side of the shell, his hand cut by the thorny protrusions along the rim. He kept his grip and hacked at the turtle's head again. The blade bounced off. He had hit the bony ridge along the beast's brow. The jaws snapped again and again. Hungry rage hissed from the turtle's throat.

"Shit!" The squire took another wild swing and missed the thrashing head completely.

The beast re-oriented itself and charged away from the tree. Jonas kept his grip as best he could. Green-brown water shot up both sides of the shell, as the snapping turtle barrelled into the closest pool. In desperation, Jonas took his sword in both hands and set the point against the turtle's thick neck. With all his weight he leaned down, steel piercing flesh.

The snapping turtle bellowed and thrashed its head. Jonas was flung through the air, his hands slipping from the sword hilt. He landed in water, choking his way to the surface.

The turtle continued to bellow, jaws snapping in agitation. The squire saw that his sword was still lodged in the base of its neck. The beast turned in a steady circle, yellow eyes searching for the source of its pain.

Jonas felt a surge of pity. He considered slipping away while the creature was confused -- but his sword gleamed. What was he without his good steel? *Bleeding in minutes, dead in hours.* His master's words.

SPELL/SWORD

"Shit," the squire said again.

He took a big breath and looked at the wounded beast carefully. It was turning in a steady clockwise circle, moaning. He timed it carefully, then ran through the shallow pool. Green water gave way to black carapace as his boots hit the turtle's shell. He kept his momentum, his arms out for balance as he ran up the living hill. His eyes focused on the bright metal ahead. Jonas stumbled but managed to fling both arms around the weapon's cross brace. The snapping turtle bellowed and the squire's veins turned to acid. Using the burst of fear, he wrapped both legs around the vast neck of the turtle and pushed down on the sword's hilt with all of his strength.

The beast's guttural hiss was cut short, and its head fell forward into the pool - green water splashing. Its legs went slack, and the vast shell came down. The snapping turtle gave a few final strangled moans, then was quiet.

Jonas opened his eyes and found himself still alive. He braced his feet on the turtle's neck, and pulled his good steel free. The blade was filthy with green water and black blood, but unbroken. The squire wiped it clean on his sodden cloak and smiled. He realized he'd broken a tooth and spat it out onto the turtle's shell.

Then he remembered.

He turned and looked towards the center of the marsh. Jonas sheathed his sword and climbed again onto the top of the turtle's shell. He scanned the sky for any sign of the mage's blue flight.

"Shit," he whispered.

A stone. A gray stone on the edge of a rotting log. Her hand in a thin pool of green water.

Rime was alone in her library. She pressed herself against the windows -- she pushed with all of her will.

A stone. A gray stone on the edge of a rotting log. It wasn't coming any closer.

Her hand in a thin pool of green water. It wasn't moving.

Rime turned from the windows and sat on her stool. A few numbers floated in the air above her head, giving off a faint green light. It was enough to make out the shapes of the books around her but not enough to read the text.

This had never happened before. She had spent plenty of time here, in the library of her mind. A quiet place, a safe place.

When she used her magic, it sapped her body's strength until she fell unconscious. A deep, dreamless sleep proportional to the amount of power she had used. She had been working on an exact formula for months, but the variables were too difficult to codify and she had been unsuccessful.

But never like this. Trapped inside her mind, like being shut in the attic of a dark house. No lights to read by and out the window her body would not answer.

Even the beasts in the dark were quiet. That had never happened before, not once.

Rime was terrified.

The girl forced her hands to unclench and reached out for

SPELL/SWORD

a book. She flipped to a random page. If she leaned close she could make out a few words here and there by the fluttering green number-light.

Rime closed the book. It was pointless. She compelled her hands to lay quiet and relaxed on the book's cover as she stared straight ahead into nothing.

The magic had felt so good as she soared through the air. Hours of the tiny trickle keeping her mobile, like a drizzle of sweet honey across her lips. And then to finally stop holding back. To throw herself into the storm of power.

Like being a god.

Her left index finger curled on the edge of the book. A hypothesis. Perhaps the prolonged use of her magic at such a low level had dilated her normal synaptic response. Her unconsciousness was a fail-safe: the mind shutting down for safety when it couldn't handle the flow any more. A valve twisting shut. On/Off. What if her control wasn't so binary? Controlling the tiny flow for so long resulted in an incomplete shutdown. Or perhaps her mind was growing resistant to the magic's deleterious effects? The mage steepled her hands on top of the book, a sense of confidence returning.

One of the floating numbers fizzled and went out. She thought it had been a 5.

Confidence drained away. Another hypothesis. She was dying.

These would be the final moments before her mind unwound and fell into darkness. Her power had finally killed her.

Rime stood up and laid the book down on the stool, taking great care that the edges of the book did not hang off the side of the seat. She smoothed the front of her tunic and walked back to the windows of her eyes.

If this was to be the final candle-flame of her mind, she would use it looking out.

She folded her hands and looked out the windows at the gray stone. At the rotting log, and her hand in the puddle. The sun was moving toward the horizon, long shadows stretching from every tree and stand of reeds. Rime knew most of the animal life in the Wheelbrake was nocturnal. *If some rodent starts chewing on my hand ... will I feel it?*

She watched a drop of water roll slowly down her motionless hand, bending and weaving along the fine lines of her skin.

The sun sank and the shadow grew longer. Rime was starting to get bored.

At least death should be interesting.

The mage walked carefully around the room and collected the fading green numbers. She hooked them carefully together into a tidy bundle of arithmetic and light. Rime flipped her book back open and held the light close in her other hand.

Just enough light to read. Rime nodded with satisfaction.

It was a book on the construction of musical instruments, **Trumpets of Eridia: Their Manufacture, History, Legacy and Subtle Beauty** by Flaubert I.

The girl sighed and settled in to wait for sundown.

SPELL/SWORD

A noise -- more a vibration than a true sound. Rime looked up from her book.

The sun had almost set, making it difficult to see out of the windows. Something was moving. Water rippled as something large approached.

Brown fabric nearly covered her vision, but she could see her body rise. She stared through the windows at the filthy face of Jonas. He was saying something and shaking her in consternation.

Rime went back to reading the terrible book about trumpets.

Jonas flopped the mage's limp form onto the bank and laid his ear against her chest. He held his breath and listened.

...thump...thump...

Her heart was still beating. The squire looked her over. She didn't appear to be bleeding, and her chest rose and fell. Her skin was even paler than normal; a shock of bone-white hair had appeared at her temple. The squire touched it with curiosity; it felt just like regular hair.

The squire shut his eyes for a moment and let himself breathe. He had half-trotted through the marsh following the direction of Rime's flight -- but when he had spotted her small body flopped unceremoniously in a small puddle he had thought the worst.

His eyes popped open, and he looked towards the setting sun. Not much light left, and he had no idea where he was.

He carefully bound the mage's hands again, and slid her onto his back. *Wild mage for a backpack.* Jonas grinned, pushing the leather satchel from Jericho to the side to make room for her.

The only choice that made sense was to keep going the way that the mage had been flying. She needed help, and Jonas knew he was no doctor. The Gray Witch, if she existed, was the mage's only hope.

The squire got his bearings and headed further into the center of the Wheelbrake. Rime's head lolled against his shoulder, nerveless as a doll's.

17

In the center of the swamp was a lake. It backed up against a giant square obelisk too even to be naturally formed. Jonas squinted across the still waters of the lake, faded shapes and symbols between the moss. The sun was almost gone, peeking through the treeline to the west. The carvings were unrecognizable, alien and strange. The squire was certain that Rime would have recognized them immediately. The giant stone block towered over the lake, a stop-wall against the marsh. A small spit of land made a beach at the obelisk's edge, and then he saw the shell-house.

The obelisk was strange, but the shell-house was lunacy. A house fashioned from a giant sea-shell. Smoke rose from a tidy chimney, and a clothes line ran from two birch poles in the yard. Damp white sheets hung heavy on the line. His eyes kept flicking between the ordinary features of the house, and the burnished rose exterior of the giant conch. A green wooden door and plain windows with thick glass was set into the slow spiral of the conch. There was a mailbox.

Painted on the mailbox in red letters was *THE Gray Witch*. The first word very clearly emphasized.

Jonas sat down. It was the mailbox. That broke him.

The comatose mage's head flopped back as he sat, and the squire quickly leaned forward to keep her neck from injury. Rime's forehead came to rest on his shoulder again. Her condition pushed him forward, edging around the still waters of the lake.

The water was shallow between the shore and the obelisk; Jonas sloshed through, noticing brightly colored fish darting away from his boots. He crossed onto the witch's beach, yellow sand giving way beneath his feet. The squire moved carefully along the rim of the beach and approached the shell-house using a footpath of black stones that lead directly up to the front door. Jonas had no experience in dealing with witches, but he assumed that they wouldn't take kindly to a stranger tromping through their linen on the line.

The squire knocked on the green door. This close the rose-colored conch seemed a darker red, especially at the center of the spiral. His blood was that color.

He waited, his stomach tight. He knocked again, a little louder.

"Around back," a voice called. "In the garden."

Jonas jumped back from the door and nearly dropped the unconscious mage in his haste. He forced himself to stop and turned back towards the house. The squire straightened his back with military crispness and stalked around the side of the house. He realized that his right hand was trying to smooth his hair down and pulled it

SPELL/SWORD

away with his left. Something in the voice, a note of authority, mother-father-grandmother-instructor-shopkeep tone that made his knees shake.

Behind the shell-house was the largest wooden tub the squire had ever seen. It was knee-height and as wide as a parade ground and filled to the brim with black earth. A lazy oval overflowing with flowers, beans, potato vines, two crisp lines of corn, and tidy rows of green peas. Placed in the middle of the giant bucket-garden was a white chair with its back towards him. A wide-brimmed red hat was all he could see of the chair's occupant.

"Jonas of Gilead, murderer and runaway, tripping through my tulips and stomping on my peas!" the red hat shifted slightly in his direction. "What a strange day, what a holiday tune. Come forward, sellsword, and meet the Gray Witch of Wheelbrake Marsh."

The witch stood up and turned to face him. Her skin was as gray as a funeral slab, the edge of a storm. She was completely nude under her bright red hat, and it took a moment for Jonas to notice her eyes - sharp, brown and human. The squire flushed and stared down at his boots, crusted with yellow sand.

"Oh, so modest! You expected perhaps some old crone? All warty and stirring a cauldron? Look at me, boy." The witch's voice was a whip.

Jonas jerked his head up, and Rime's dead weight flopped back again. He was abruptly terrified. That voice could tell him to do anything -- jump off a cliff, cut off his own hand, rip out a child's eyes -- and he would obey. He would obey without question.

"Place your burden here. *Doma* Korvanus has been a

193

potato sack for quite long enough today," she said, pointing to her chair.

The squire swung Rime's unconscious form around and sat her down gently in the chair. The Gray Witch crossed her arms and laid a long gray finger against her cheek. She peered down at Rime the way a matron considers apples at the market.

She tossed her red hat to Jonas. He caught it and was surprised to find that it was made of simple straw. The witch's sweat was damp on the band.

The Gray Witch's face was an inch from Rime's. "Yes, I can see you in there little wildling. Getting dark, isn't it?"

The witch's eyes speared Jonas. "She will die. Soon. Do not crease my hat, please." Her attention returned to the mage's slack face.

"Burned to a cinder. Wasteful. You showed much promise, *Doma* Rime. And now here you are, pathetic and broken," The witch cocked her head slightly, as if listening. "Yes, I know why you've come here, I know what you would ask. But you arrive with nothing to offer, and the Gray Witch does nothing for nothing. Hmmm?"

There was another pause, and then the witch began to laugh. Her laugh was thick and sliding, seeming to come from everywhere at once.

"Take the boy? You trade him twice before sunset? Twice for your own life? Interesting..." The witch turned her brown eyes on the squire. "Very well. For sunset and water, for dream and blood... and because it pleases me to do so."

SPELL/SWORD

Two long gray hands twined around the mage's face and down the front of her tunic. The witch's hands curled into the fabric and lifted the small girl's body into the air. Casually, she threw her out across the lake with the ease of a small boy tossing a stone. Rime's body spun with the force and landed flat on the water. Her cloak billowed out in the water, slowing her descent. Jonas turned immediately to follow, dropping the witch's hat.

"Stop," the witch said.

And Jonas did.

"Pick up my hat and bring it here."

And Jonas did.

Her brown eyes burned, most terrifying for how ordinary they looked, even in her slate-gray face. She placed the hat lightly on the chairback and ran a finger down the squire's filthy cheek.

Rime is going to die. Rime is going to die. I have to move, but I can't move. She won't LET me move. Rime is going to die. Rime is going to die.

"Yes," the witch said. "She is."

The Gray Witch idly scratched the stubble on his cheek.

"Rime is a selfish child, and she will die as soon as the sun sets. Bare minutes from now. Choke on green water and die. But she has offered you up to save her. A simple trade, she thought. But what fun would that be? Let us be traditional."

The witch sprawled back in her chair and closed her eyes.

195

"A knight and his lady... and a witch. Yes, it must be the old way." Her eyes popped open. "I will ask you three questions. If you answer them correctly, I will aid the wild mage. Answer them poorly, and she will die."

Jonas felt her voice pull back slightly; he was a tiny bird in a cat's claws. Just enough room to flap and chirp, not enough to fly away.

"Uhhhh... okay?" he said, heroically.

Rime pushed against the windows of her eyes and watched the green water rise outside. She held the faintly glowing numerals tight in her fist, squashed against the glass. She could just barely hear the witch and the squire's conversation. Her face twisted in frustration. She grabbed a thought-cable from near the window and smashed it into the center of the green numbers. Some quick reorientation of a few numbers and she crafted a crude radio. It crackled, but the voices were more audible.

...swer them poorly and she will die."

"Uhhhh....okay?"

Rime slammed her forehead against the glass and gritted her teeth.

"Why did you save her?" the witch asked.

SPELL/SWORD

Jonas furrowed his brow. "Uhh, is this the first question? I thought it would be more like a riddle, or--"

The witch said nothing, but flicked her eyes towards the setting sun.

"She needed my help," Jonas replied.

Flat brown eyes. "She left you to die."

"Look, it wasn't like that. I'm sure she was going to circle back and hit that turtle from behind, but she ran out of juice and crashed."

"She left you. To die."

The squire felt sick to his stomach. He knew the witch wasn't lying. He had thought it himself as he searched for the mage, but had let it fall out of his head.

"Well, I'm sure she felt like she had no choice," Jonas said. "It's my job to protect her anyway."

"Correct answer: You are an idiot," the witch said. "Next question. When will you die?"

The squire's mouth fell open. "How am I supposed to... I don't know..."

He felt the claws tightening again.

"I really want to tell you what you want to hear," he said, waving his hands in agitation, "But how could I possibly know that? The Nameless will call me home when my work is done, that's what we learned in church. If I had to guess, it would probably be after doing something very, very stupid."

"Correct answer: Never."

"What?" Jonas said, reeling. "What does that mean?"

The witch smiled a quiet, terrible smile. "My questions, not yours. Last question."

The wind sang across the pool, and Jonas could hear the quiet bubbling of Rime's body sinking. The golden sun grew dim. He desperately wanted to say something, but the witch's face was gray stone.

"Will you kiss me?" she said.

The squire started to speak, then stopped. He pointed at the witch, then at himself, then made an indistinct whirling gesture with both hands.

The witch smiled again and held her arms wide.

Jonas pushed the hair out of his face, a red flush going up his neck. He tried to think. *I've already gotten two questions wrong, I've got to get this one right!* He turned quickly and saw that Rime was nearly underwater, only her nostrils and mouth above the green water.

Wasting no more time, he approached the Gray Witch. He knelt over her chair and lowered his face towards her. Her brown eyes gave nothing away, and her gray flesh may as well have been stone. She moved not at all.

Her lips parted, and she said, "Correct answer: No."

Then she grabbed the back of his head and pulled his lips to hers.

Her lips were gray and her tongue was gray and her teeth were gray and she breathed gray into his lungs and the gray was in him. But her mouth was hot and wet, and he wept because he could taste that she was still human, somewhere underneath it all.

Jonas wept, and the gray was in him.

18

Rime woke up. She didn't remember falling asleep.

She wasn't in her library anymore. She was someplace new. A cozy red blanket covered her, and she was suspended in some sort of hammock. Green framed windows opened into cricket-sound night. The White Moon was still full, and the Red and Black tiny slivers. Not more than a day could have passed.

The room was very small, and the walls curved strangely. She looked right and saw a narrow staircase spiralling downwards.

Rime realized she was inside the witch's shell-house.

She reached up to pull the blanket carefully away and was surprised to discover her hands not moving. Her head shook weakly back and forth with the strain, but the rest of her body refused to answer. Rime stared up at the curved ceiling and felt her eyes begin to water. Something moved under the hammock.

The Gray Witch sat up and laid her chin on the mage's shoulder. The hammock bobbed slightly. *She was laying...on the floor?* The mage bit her tongue, pain and copper slid down her throat.

The witch blinked. "Feeling better are we?"

"Yes." Rime replied, her voice thin. *I will not give her... the satisfaction of being surprised.*

"I saved you. Soon you will sleep again. Leave your magic alone for a moon's turn, at least." The witch's face appeared massive in Rime's view, chin a sharp weight on her shoulder.

"What happened to me?"

"Drank too much water. Your vessel can only hold so much, little wild mage. I had to wring all of it out of you. " the witch's hands crept up on either side of the hammock and gave Rime a little squeeze. "Drip, drip, drip. All the wild magic squeezed right out of you, so your silly little heart could remember how to beat. Now say what you are thinking, Rime Korvanus."

"You... you are not a wild mage. I thought you were." Rime made her voice stay steady. "You can't help me... learn... learn how not to go insane."

The witch laughed and laid back down on the floor. The Gray Witch chuckled and batted Rime's hammock back and forth like a lazy cat. The mage felt her whole body vibrate as the witch's words rose through her.

"Not a wild mage, no. Not a wizard, so. Not a farmer, la.

201

Not a charmer, ha!" the witch sang. "I am a piece of the Old stuck in the New. Strange and stranger, dog in the manger! Bark - bark!"

"Or it happened while I was asleep. This is insanity." Rime said, growing dizzy.

The witch's gray hands slipped away, and the hammock's swinging slowed. Her voice continued at a more normal pitch.

"All this way, burning yourself and everything you touch. Corpses and blood. Was it worth it, *Doma*?"

"That's an absurd question. I accomplished nothing," Rime said. "I'm going to go mad and die, just like every other wild mage."

The mage's words tumbled from her lips like heavy black stones, and they pooled on her chest and started spilling off the hammock. They clinked on the floor as they fell.

There it was. The truth she'd been avoiding for months, for years, for the days on the trail, through Talbot and the Drift Canyon and Jericho and the Wheelbrake. Ever since she'd learned the truth of her nature, she'd searched through her father's library for something that could save her. The tales of the Gray Witch, appearing in so many cultural traditions, across a span of so many years, a figure of immense power, of terrible knowledge. Why had she come to the conclusion that the witch must be a wild mage? It had seemed so certain, the best solution she had found after months of research. Now it seemed foolish. A half-baked theory.

"Well, maybe not 'just' like every other wild mage." Rime could feel the witch's long finger tracing the curve of her back through the canvas of the hammock. "You assume that because I am not a wild mage that I have no knowledge of them."

The girl's head jerked up. "What knowledge?"

"Nothing for nothing, little girl," the witch replied. "What do you have to offer?"

Jonas. The name fluttered into view, making slow circles around her toe. The witch chuckled again, and Rime's heart shook.

"Three times before the cock crows? Thrice paid by the son of Gilead? Come now, child. Don't flog a dead horse."

Jonas. Dead. The first word stopped circling as the second appeared. They sailed to meet each other and hung like constellations at the foot of her bed. Rime felt an unfamiliar sensation.

"What do you want? Don't toy with me, like that fool. You seem to know everything, you know what I'm capable of. You know what I've done to get here. Don't dance around, witch, tell me your price. Tell me quick, you're boring me," Rime said, her fist clenched in the red blanket, hot unnoticed tears seared down her face.

The hammock suddenly was turned upside down. The witch gripped her shoulders, mild eyes calm. Thin gray fingers dug into bone, and the mage's joints howled. Rime stared down into the terrible brown eyes of the Gray Witch and screamed.

"Do not test me, child. I am the last of what was; after me there will be no others. You say you are no fool? Then I will speak plain. The boy has paid for your life, the cost most dear." The Gray Witch's voice was quiet. "There is nothing in this world that you can offer me. Nothing that I desire. You have nothing to buy this knowledge from me."

Rime choked back a sob and had to admit to herself that she was crying. *Tears… I haven't.. .done this… since I was small… how dare this creature… Jonas.. .you stupid…*

The witch let her fall from the hammock and pulled her close, still swaddled in the red blankets. She whispered in Rime's ear. "Shhh… that boy has a heart of silver. Not as precious as gold but more true. There is no shame in weeping for him."

Rage coursed through her, but she couldn't stop sobbing. The witch ran gravestone fingers through her hair.

"You will go to Gilead, to the throne of the King. There you will find your answer." The witch's voice was strange, like a light dimming. "We will never meet again. In time you will know my price."

The girl felt darkness sliding over her; the witch's strange gray face began to fall away.

"The Knight waits for you at the edges of this swamp. You must defeat him, or your journey ends today."

Brown, human eyes blinked into Rime's.

"And in time you will know the cost. Ah, your tears are cold, but his were oh so sweet."

The witch was gone, but her voice remained, quiet and gray.

"Oh, the end is so black. So dark and black. If I

remembered how, I would weep, but I don't, I don't. Weary wind and songs of the lost... as the seasons turn you will know... the end is so, so black."

Rime was alone in the darkness, and she fell into the easier abyss of sleep.

The sun was hot on Rime's face, and she woke up again.

She was laying on a sandy spit next to a still green lake. Sitting up, she saw the shadow of the giant carved obelisk across the lake. The witch's shell-house was gone, as if it had never been there.

A thick groan came from behind her, and she leaped up to defend herself, as her muscles screamed in complaint. She pulled the small dagger from her belt and stared at a ghost.

Jonas was laying face down in the mud. He groaned for another moment, then pushed himself up slowly. Lake algae and particles of sand stuck to his face and matted his hair. He looked around blearily and spotted her. The squire grinned, showing white teeth.

"That was..." he coughed up a cupful of green water and continued weakly. "That was my first kiss."

19

The squire and the mage sat back to back on the sandy shore. By the sun, it was still early morning. The day promised to be hot; the earthy stench of the marsh began to rise, the hum of cicadas a low rumble. Rime had helped pull the squire out of the lake's edge, finding her body capable if creaky. The squire rooted around in the battered leather satchel he still carried and pulled out the last of their provisions: a thin twist of goat jerky. Jonas sawed at it with the mage's dagger and passed half to Rime. It was tough; the satchel would have tasted better.

"So," Rime said finally.

"Yeah?"

"Not dead then?"

"Nope."

"Well," Rime said. "I wasn't going to come back for you."

"I know," Jonas said.

Rime chewed ferociously on the stub of jerky. How could

SPELL/SWORD

he be so calm about it? "I'll do it again. If it's between my life or yours, I'll pick mine every time."

"Okay."

"Okay? Okay?!?" The mage stood up, and wheeled around to face him. "What kind of idiot are you? Don't you have any sense of self-preservation? Do you have a death wish?"

"Look, Rime... I... I don't know, okay?" Jonas stood up and faced the mage. "The witch made me think about a lot of things. I guess it's just... look. I've run away from my home, a lot of responsibilities. And now, it's my job --"

"Your job to what? To die? To die nobly at my side?" The young girl's face was taut with anger. *Why am I so angry? Why?*

"You're my friend, and dying to keep you safe is much better than getting stabbed in a bar, or rotting in a cell somewhere!" Jonas yelled. "I'm your guardian."

"My guardian?" Rime retorted. "Let me be absolutely clear. I don't care anything about your life. You're basically a horse that carries a sword. I will ride you into the ground, and continue on when you fall."

Rime watched the words take shape in the air, obsidian-razor and a strange shade of purple. She wanted to take them back, no matter how they cut her. But she could not. They were true, of course, but she didn't want him to hear them.

Jonas stared at her seriously, his face a picture of confusion. Abruptly, his face cleared. "Nah. Not really. You won't do that."

"I won't?" Rime said quietly.

"My master told me again and again. We choose how we see the world, and we choose how we walk in it. I'm your guardian, Rime, and you're my friend." His thick face shone with sincerity.

The mage was stunned at the boy's willful stupidity. Her mind drew in the air above his head, a scribble of Jonas stacking thick logs to hide the truth from himself, building a wall. Her words bounced off his stubborn wall and spun off into the air. The ink-Jonas was whistling, slapping fresh mortar on the logs, to make sure they were all but immovable. She looked down into the squire's face and saw the pride there.

Jonas slid his sword out of the sheath, and held it flat in both hands. He offered the blade out to her. "I swear by my good steel, that I will defend you, Rime Korvanus. As long as it takes, wherever the road takes us. It's all that I have left, the only thing that will make me matter in this world."

Rime rolled her eyes, "This is absurd."

She ignored the sword and pushed Jonas hard in the stomach.

"Ooof," he said, taking a step back, but still holding his sword out.

In frustration, she took it and looked down at it. It was plain and unremarkable. There had to be thousands in the world just like it.

Swords. Such simple things. A sharpened bit of metal, with wood on one end to hold onto. They have one purpose, and one meaning. But

208

so much weight is heaped onto them -- in every tale, in endless songs. This one stands for Justice, and this one stands for Truth, and this dark blade is the Key of Evil, and this one turns into a carrot when the princess wiggles her nose. And this one is....

She smiled, just a little. *This one is my friend's sword.*

Rime gave Jonas back his sword. He looked at her uncertainly.

"Let's go then... *guardian.*" Her tone was frosty. "We need to get out of this swamp, and I have to decide how we're going to deal with that Hunter and his men. The witch warned me that they are watching the edges of the swamp."

"The witch warned you? What else did she say?"

"Nothing important," Rime lied.

The two travelers crouched behind a low dune covered with scrub bushes. They had used up most of the day making their way to the marsh's northern edge. Rime had explained: "They have the advantage of numbers and mobility, their wyverns can easily cover the perimeter of the marsh with regular patrols. They know we have to leave at some point, and once they spot us, it will take them a matter of moments to send word and swarm us. On open ground we'll never lose them. We need to come out of the marsh at the point where they would be least likely to be looking: the northern edge, right against the ocean. They will assume that we have no way to escape by sea and concentrate their patrols elsewhere."

"Wait.. do we have a way to escape by sea? Can you turn yourself into a boat?"

"What? No," Rime had sighed and continued. "Why would you even think I could... never mind, I don't want to know."

"I don't know how you wild mages work," Jonas complained.

"The point is, it's our best chance of exiting the marsh undetected. We'll slip along the coast, moving east until we can make a break to the south and disappear into the forest."

The smell of the sea had grown stronger as they travelled north, the brackish green pools and clumps of rotting logs mixing with blown white sand. The murmur of the waves grew in their ears. A green pool gave way to slow-moving stream. A low dune curved around to the right. Jonas and Rime sloshed up onto the sandy beach and followed the curve of the dune towards the edge of the ocean.

The mage hissed a warning, and pulled the squire's head down as they rounded the bend. A blue pavilion stood whipping in the wind, two wyverns were tethered to iron spikes just beyond.

"What are they doing here?" Jonas whispered.

Rime didn't answer, her mind putting on its armor. *Two wyverns. Command center. Probability that they would be here, 10-15%. Bad luck or some other variable. Some method of tracking us? Unlikely. They would have swooped in on us while we were defenseless in the marsh.* Her vision filled with lines and numbers, shapes twisting and forming as she frantically redid her calculations.

210

SPELL/SWORD

The flap of the blue pavilion twitched, and the blonde wizard from Jericho stepped into view. Even from this distance, they could see her eyes blazing yellow in the late afternoon shadows.

The blonde woman turned and said something in the direction of the pavilion. The dark-clad assassin with the mangled horns appeared, followed by the knight in iron armor. Rime looked immediately for the white sword and found it sheathed at the knight's hip. The old man's face was calm as he gestured to the devil-kin at his side.

The assassin cupped his hands around his mouth and bellowed. "Come on! We know you're out there."

Rime's calculations folded in on themselves and disappeared. It didn't matter now. She spoke quickly to the squire as she stood up. "They've got us out-classed. You're no match for their sword-fighter, but can you keep him busy for a few minutes?"

"Uh... I guess? I got the feeling he was being polite before."

"Fine. We'll move in and see what they have to say... any chance of an advantage. I'll concentrate on their wizard while you keep the devil-kin off my back. Once she's dead, I'll finish off the assassin." *Leave your magic alone for a moon's turn, at least.* The witch's words burned.

"Okay. What about the guy with the sword that sucks up all your magic?" Jonas said.

Rime narrowed her eyes. "I have an idea..."

211

Linus watched the two ragged children make their way across the beach. They were wet and covered with muck from their armpits down -- reeds and sand stuck in their hair. The old man took a slow breath of sea air.

There are worse places than this to meet one's end. Linus drew the white sword and stabbed it firmly into the earth in front of him, then clasped both iron gauntlets around the hilt. "Just as you predicted, Ms. Belaine," he said.

Cotton nodded, the yellow light fading from her eyes. "They will speak with us first, then attack. The boy will fall easily, then we can focus on the abomination."

"Spare the boy if you can," Linus said.

"Sure, he seems like a decent kid," Sideways replied, pulling free his scorched blade.

The old knight focused his attention on the two bedraggled children and pitched his voice to be heard over the wind. "Hail and well met, travelers!"

The girl stopped, her face twisting like lemon-taste. The boy drew his sword and held it in a serviceable defensive posture. Linus quirked an eyebrow. *Some training there.*

A scant fifty yards separated them from their quarry. His blade and his wizard were perfectly still, waiting for his command. The old man felt the weight of his armor, and the sea-air smelled like grief.

"How did you know we'd be here?" the girl demanded.

"Such poor manners, *Doma* Korvanus. Nary an introduction?" The knight gestured, "It is here at the edge of the world that the tenets of civilization must be

212

SPELL/SWORD

observed most closely. It is my pleasure to present Ms. Cotton Belaine, a seer and prophet of some note. Her talents lead us to pitch our pavilion here. Prudence keeps the remainder of my men patrolling the southern border of the Marsh most carefully."

"A seer?" the girl said, her face going still.

"Like, she can see the future?" the boy said, letting his guard slip slightly. Linus fought the urge to correct the young man, a thousand hours in the practice yard leave their mark. "Then how did we get away the first time?"

"Not now," the girl said.

"But... I don't..." he continued.

"Later," she hissed at him.

"I like these two," the devil-kin smirked.

"And this is Sideways, our 'scout'." Linus smiled at the small joke. "And I am Linus, once called Linus the Blue, Linus the Spellbreaker, Gray-Fog Finder and Steelbiter. I am the last of the great Hunt, and it has fallen to me to bring you down, wild mage. For the safety of Aufero and so you may avoid the black spiral of madness that is your heritage. Out of respect for your family and for your youth, I wish to offer you the chance to surrender. I would have done so in Jericho if you had not departed in such haste."

"Surrender. So you can put me in a cage?" the girl sneered.

"No, my dear. But I can promise you a swift and painless death. And of course the life of your companion will be spared." The knight pointed an iron finger.

213

"No deal," the boy said stoutly. The girl nodded.

Linus sighed. "Very well. Cotton, Sideways pl--"

"Now!" the girl yelled, and thick green spikes erupted from the sand. They were no thicker than a quill, but they stretched twenty, thirty feet in the air, and bent back over the pavilion, making an effective cage. Linus and the blonde wizard were inside, the assassin was outside.

The boy charged forward to engage Sideways, and the girl's hands glowed with thin blue light.

A clever ploy. Linus pulled the sword free from the sand and swung a lazy half-moon arc. The green spikes sizzled and burned, cut and absorbed by the white sword. Cotton nodded and stepped through the opening, her eyes erupting with yellow light.

Rime's diversion had bought her about five seconds.

Five seconds is a long time. A lot can happen in five seconds: a heart can break, a life can end, a baby can take its first breath. Rime drew a clock in glowing purple ink and made her mind go faster.

In one second Jonas would intercept the craggy-horned assassin. She used that second to complete her assessment of the terrain. Coarse yellow sand running down to the ocean at low tide. No cover, they had the clear advantage in numbers and battle prowess. The sand had some possibilities. It was granular and heavy, but the thought of manipulating that much soil made her quail.

Jonas and the devil-kin were moving in slow motion, the latter's gray mouth wide as he shouted a command to his sword. "Sunhammer!" The scorched blade ignited with red flame, and the squire managed a clumsy parry. *Magic sword. Problem.*

Two seconds from now the hunter's white sword would shear through her flimsy cage. One second after that the seer would be outside the cage, and she would have to fight for her life. Rime allotted one second for planning and one second for pain.

The leather-clad devil-kin presented little problem. Their earlier encounter on the bridge showed him to only be an effective physical combatant. Kept at a distance he could be dispensed with efficiently with a few well placed blasts of her magic. The blonde wizard was a much greater threat. Rime's knowledge of seers and prophets was not extensive, but from the evidence available the woman clearly had a limited ability to predict the course of future events. *Strategy?* The little purple clock chirped, and Rime had no answer. As to her combat ability, surely the Hunt would not bring along any wizard who couldn't hold their own on the battlefield. *Strategy?* The purple clock in her mind's eye chirped again, second hand ticking forward. *I need to keep her as far from that white sword as possible. It can counter all my attacks. Other than that?*

Rime had no answer, because it was time to give herself over to the pain. Just for a second.

whitehoticeneedlesinmyskinonmyskintheachingteethofwhitehoticeneedles inmyskinonmyskin

A second can be a long time.

215

Her magic hurt. It was still there, as abundant and eager as ever, but channeling it was agony. Like walking on a dislocated ankle, or chewing with broken teeth. Sharp and clear and bright, blood-simple and razor-edged. Rime had tried to use the tiniest amount possible by making the bars of the green cage thin and brittle. But it still hurt, and it was making it harder and harder to think. The mage's thoughts edged over slightly into her final second out of pure terror. Her mind was her only weapon, and it was proving dull when she needed it most.

Her eyes flicked to the squire's back. Jonas was giving ground as the assassin's flaming sword spun and collided with the squire's plain steel. But he was holding, for now.

The blonde wizard stepped through the broken cage, and her yellow eyes blazed. Rime banished the clock and banished the pain.

Five seconds were up.

A lot can go wrong in five seconds.

Jonas had tried to keep a stoic look on his face when the red sword erupted in front of him. It had happened before, and he was expecting it. His first parry had been a little slow but effective. He met the next few blows solid and clean, the panic-knot in his chest loosened ever so slightly. He would do his part and trust in Rime to do hers. He could certainly keep the assassin busy for half a minute or more.

Then he saw the coral-horned devil yawn -- slowly and theatrically, raising the back of his free hand to his mouth.

SPELL/SWORD

The assassin's other hand held the flaming sword loosely, but his blows were fierce and rapid.

"What's the deal? Are you just playing with me?" Jonas grunted.

"Oh no, you're doing a good job, kid," Sideways said, flipping the sword to his opposite hand, then bringing it crashing down onto the squire's panicked overhand block. "Good technique -- somebody trained you right. You're going to be a pretty fair sword-slinger. Assuming that I don't kill you shortly."

The assassin kicked sand into the squire's eyes. Jonas clawed them clean with enough time to block the next lunge from the devilkin, but his foot caught in the sand, forcing him to make an awkward stumble to the right. The squire rolled forward and kicked himself up off the ground. Sideways was sliding closer, a regretful expression on his slanted face.

The squire saw out of the corner of his eye the lady wizard stepping out of the cage.

"Sorry, kid, time to shut it down." Sideways drew a line in the sand with his flaming sword. The yellow sand turned instantly to black glass. "Now bring your best -- don't be shy."

The devil-kin smiled, as friendly as a cat.

This guy is going to kill me. Jonas saluted the assassin with his good steel, blade to brow. Sideways mockingly returned the gesture. *This guy is going to kill me.*

Rime spun her magic into needles of ice -- it only seemed appropriate to use the shape of her pain. Thin little shards of magic, easier to control and maintain. They floated above her hands until she sent the first barrage forward to pierce the blonde wizard with the honey-blaze eyes.

The wizard had already moved, somersaulting to the right an instant before the needles reached her. They slid into the sand and dissolved. Cotton continued to approach, moving swiftly along the sand, her hands moving in a series of half-moon gestures, fingers bending and twisting. Rime was already sending the next burst of needles from her left hand, one needle at a time, arcing in front of the wizard, trying to pin her.

The wizard seemed to dance. A foot moving a split second before the needle caught her, shoulder bending just so, flowing from one movement to the next, a pirouette turning into a crouch. Each movement reacting to the first attack, predicting the next and leaving her in the perfect position to evade the next series. Cotton was only fifty paces away, and Rime could see the tight confident smile underneath her storm-lantern eyes.

Predict this, bitch. Rime took a quick fistful of her magic, and wind howled across the beach, clawing a gouge across the sand -- a horizontal whirlwind ripping towards the wizard. Cotton leaped high into the air, the sandstorm making her blonde hair fly, but otherwise unharmed. The wizard was coming straight down towards a patch of sand a short twenty paces from Rime. The mage grinned and pushed up with her free hand.

A giant red mouth appeared, flat square teeth chomping eagerly. It was a cow, Apple the Average, one of Rime's favorite stories as a child. The poorly drawn cow was

218

determined to succeed at every endeavor, even though she wasn't particularly bright. Cotton was inches from the creature's floppy mouth when her hands completed the spell.

The wizard vanished, and the red cow chomped down on empty air. *She knew. She saw the whirlwind and knew that it was a feint for my next attack.* This thought spiralled through Rime's vision, red-pink and thick with clotted horror.

The wizard was behind her. A snarled incantation and a prickle of heat on her neck was the only warning she had. Rime's magic thought for her, and she flew, vomit-sick worms curling through her veins. She flew in a swift arc a dozen paces away and turned in time to see the ball of fire erupt from Cotton's fingertips and land where she had been standing -- a perfect square of cherry-red flame. The two swordsmen stopped their fight briefly and shaded their eyes in amazement. The knight with his white sword watched impassively. Square flame subsided, leaving a perfect geometry of ash in the sand. Jonas and Sideways whistled in unison, then abashedly returned to their duel. Rime saw through the drowsy black squares in her vision that the squire's blade was moving slower and slower; his defeat would come within moments.

Cotton straightened, her basalt eyes on Rime. "This is already over, abomination. I can see every move you will make, every move you might make, all you can do is prolong the inevitable."

Rime stood very still.

"You will summon another cage, followed by a large wave of ice and then you will pierce my heart with a crimson vine of ivy," the blonde seer said. " Clever but ineffective. I will teleport out and shield myself with a skin of fire. You will forego the ivy, as I am no longer pinned down."

Rime gritted her teeth.

"Oh! A chain of blue steel erupts from the sand, binding my hands and feet. The chains grow legs: a suit of armor! It drags me to the surf and holds my head under until I stop kicking." Cotton clapped briefly. "I will fly into the air and turn myself intangible, bringing lightning down on your fiendish head."

Rime said nothing.

"Yes. I see them," Cotton said with a voice of golden triumph. "They ripple across these sands like the fingers of the wind. Every path you could take from this moment, every strategy, every ploy, all as clear and orderly as pieces on a chess board. Choose, child. Choose and meet your end."

"My end is not yours to see. You forget..." Rime's hair blew across her face. "...I am a *wild* mage."

Rime Korvanus threw off the pain like an unwelcome coat, breathed in the sea air, and opened her veins to the magic in her blood.

"What... no. You can't." Cotton's eyes burned a deeper gold, a corona of white flame spreading out. "You can't... you can't do them all!"

Rime did.

Linus took a step forward, but it was already too late.

Cotton Belaine fell and fell and fell, pieces of her littering the sand.

The wild mage stood at the epicenter of her destruction, shining for a moment as white as a winter star. Then she crumpled to her knees and toppled to the sand.

The knight felt a brief prick of sorrow at his wizard's passing. Another soldier fallen at his command. He pulled the white sword free from the sand and moved forward to finish his duty. It was well that this creature would die soon. This display of power ranked itself high amongst the mightiest wild mages he had brought down, and they were far older than this small girl.

The small girl was moving; Linus' eyes widened in shock. Her hand stretched forth, pointing towards the boy.

Jonas yelped in pain, as the flaming sword bit another chunk out of his upper leg. Whatever Rime had just done had stalled the fight between him and the devil-kin again, but the assassin had been the first to strike upon seeing his comrade fall.

"Can't play around anymore, kid," the assassin said. "Time for me to get paid."

The squire's arms were lead, his good steel black and scorched from the heat of Sunhammer. He managed one last weak parry, which the assassin blithely knocked aside. The flaming blade rose high and came down towards Jonas' head. He willed his arms to move, but they were too slow, too slow.

Time moved slower than his arms, and Jonas found the

old words in his head: a prayer.

We walk through the world only once. Only one life is given by the Nameless.

His arm felt lighter. His good steel shone bright and swung up to meet the sword of flame.

Except his good steel was now a sword of ice. It burned blue and bright, like the flames Rime left in the turtle's tree. Sideways cursed in surprise. Jonas cursed louder.

The sword pulled him to his feet and attacked the startled devil-kin. It was as light as air, and moved with a thought. The squire laughed a nervous donkey-bray. He and his good steel slashed again and again, for now it was the assassin who had to move with all his speed to block. A few passes more, blue against red, and Jonas saw it: an opening, a hesitation in the devil-kin's footwork, and he lunged.

Sunhammer spun through the air and landed flat against the sand. It smoked for a moment, then went out like a spent match. The squire's sword still rippled with blue flame and the point was held to the assassin's throat.

"Kill him," Rime croaked from across the sand, her voice low but audible. "Quick."

Jonas kept his eyes on the assassin. "No, Rime. I don't... we're not doing things that way. He fought with honor, and I'm not going to kill an unarmed man... devil ... devil-man?"

The corners of Sideways' mouth quirked in amusement, even as his hands began to slowly slide upwards. "You're all right, kid. Stupid, but all right. Your juiced sword dealt

222

SPELL/SWORD

with ol' Sunhammer just fine, but I don't think you're going to fare so well with my friend, Chet."

"Who?" the squire said uncertainly. He couldn't see Rime's expression, but he could nearly hear her eyes rolling.

"Dammit, fine." The sand beneath the assassin's feet rippled and spun. As adroitly as a hammered nail, the assassin disappeared beneath the sand, all except for his eyes and nose. The sound of muffled screams came from beneath the sand; the devil-kin's eyes rolled wildly, but his nostrils continued to pull in air.

"He can dig himself out later -- when we're long gone. Happy?" Rime's voice was thick with exhaustion. "Now, come pick me up."

The blue flame flickered and died on the sword. Jonas waggled his blade awkwardly over the devil-kin's head in an attempt at apology, then trotted across the sand to the mage's side.

Nearly a third of her hair had turned as white as snow.

"Ach, Rime, you've got to be more careful or people will start calling you grandmother before your sixteenth birthday," he said pulling her into his arms.

"What... what are you talking about?" she said.

"Your hair is... look, maybe we should talk about this later..." the squire grinned.

The crunch of sand as armored boots approached. The two travelers whipped their heads about as one.

The knight stopped, the white sword blooming from his

223

iron-clad hands.

20

The old man said nothing, the sea breeze blowing through his thinning gray hair. He did not taunt, or question, or speak one word. He only stood with the white sword in his hands and waited. The knight measured the squire and mage with his eyes. The boy stood, slightly hunched, bearing the girl's weight in his arms.

"Are you ready?" Rime asked Jonas.

"Nope," the squire said and dropped his sword to fall in the sand.

Linus watched it fall and did not move. The old hunter couldn't keep from tilting his head slightly in curiosity. A strange turn of the page.

SPELL/SWORD

Jonas reached behind Rime's back and slipped his hand inside the battered leather satchel they had carried from Jericho. With a thin grunt, he tossed Rime to the side and charged the knight. He folded the satchel around his right hand like an oven mitt. "Yaaaah!" was the best battle cry he could muster.

The knight's eyes widened in confusion, but he raised the white sword to one shoulder and swung another half-moon arc to slice the boy in half. Jonas swung his body to meet the sword, the satchel-glove opened wide.

Rime perked up blearily from the sand, and pointed an index finger at the glove. A bright yellow chicken appeared filling the palm of the glove. Its red beak let out a cheery "Caw-cu-caw!" just as the white sword hit.

The sword absorbed the arcane chicken instantly. It vanished in mid crow. The blade slowed -- just enough -- and Jonas closed the satchel over the blade and gripped with all his strength.

The squire and the knight strained against each other with the white sword between them.

Linus was sputtering, "What -- what --"

Jonas kept his grip and leaned against the sword using all his weight.

The knight was old, and the squire was young. After a few heartbeats of strain, Jonas ripped the white sword free.

He trotted a few steps away and turned back to his companion. His face was red with strain, but glowing with pride.

225

"Look, Rime, it worked! I got it! I got..." his words were cut short as Rime raised her left hand.

A wave of force like an invisible hand gripped the scruff of the squire's cloak and hauled him up in the air.

"Wha... what, Rime... what?" Jonas exclaimed.

"Drop it when you land," she said, and the invisible hand flung the squire and sword out into the waves, nearly a half mile into the blue-green water. Jonas continued to yell in protest until he landed with a distant splash.

Rime leaned on her elbow, as her legs were too weak to support her. She pointed her left hand at the knight.

Linus turned from watching the sword and squire fly through the air and nodded to the mage. "Well done. A clever strategy, I must admit. How could you be sure that the sword wouldn't absorb the force that tossed your guardian?"

"I wasn't," Rime said. "I was hoping that the sword requires a modicum of skill to operate. Jonas has none, so it seemed a fair bet, and it avoided any further argument or explanation."

"Ah," the knight smiled. "Then I am not to be honorably imprisoned in the sand, like my scout over there?"

"No," Rime said.

"Wise."

A beam of red light burst forth from her hand and punched through the knight's breastplate -- right over his

SPELL/SWORD

heart. The old man's face went slack and he toppled backwards. Rime's magic left a cruel, scorched hole in the armor; the flesh underneath smoked and sizzled. The mage pulled herself closer, hissing in pain. The knight was still and dead, but she crawled close and jabbed her belt knife in his throat for safety.

Several minutes later, Jonas swam ashore. He was soaking wet, seaweed tangled in his clothes and hair. He had dropped the white sword as instructed but had managed to sling the satchel back around his neck. *Damn thing saved our bacon, it deserves better than to sink to the bottom of the ocean.*

Rime had pulled herself up into a sitting position, cross-legged next to the recumbent form of the knight. The squire saw immediately that he was dead; a small puddle of drying blood stained the yellow sand near his neck. And the giant hole in his armor.

The girl stared out at the sea, her brown hair cut through with chalk white, blowing in the wind. "Yes, I killed him. An unarmed man."

"I see," the squire said. "There wasn't any other way?"

"He would've kept coming; you know that."

"I guess." Jonas sat down in the sand. "I guess you're right."

The waves crashed on the shore, and sea-air filled the quiet space.

"We should probably go."

"Yes. The patrols will return before long. Think you can manage to not lose the wyvern this time?"

Jonas looked over towards where the two purple beasts were tethered at the pavilion. "Well, how about you fly your own this time? And I thought we agreed to never, ever speak of that?"

"I'm going to sleep for several days. You can be pilot," Rime said. "I trust you."

The squire had already stood up before the mage's words registered. He opened his mouth to speak, but in a moment of remarkable wisdom said nothing.

"Idiot," the mage did not smile. "Now pick me up, and let's get out of here."

"Where are we going?" Jonas took the mage's hands.

"South," Rime said. "For now. Follow the coast until you hit Carroway. It's a big town, and I have some money there."

"Is the food good?" Jonas asked, but the girl was already asleep.

The squire carried his friend to the wyvern's saddle and tucked her into the back compartment. He ransacked the knight's pavilion, taking a thick wool blanket and a basket of food. "Spoils of war," he reassured himself.

Jonas munched on a thick slab of white cheese as he slid into the saddle. He crammed it all the way into his mouth so he could take the reins.

"Aghllump," he said, mouth full of cheese, and flicked the

SPELL/SWORD

reins.

The wyvern leaped into the sky, and the two travelers left the edge of the world behind.

THE END

FOR NOW

JONAS AND RIME
WILL RETURN
in
THE RIDDLE BOX

WAIT. DON'T GO YET.
TURN THE PAGE. OR YOU KNOW,
PUSH NEXT ON YOUR KINDLE OR
WHATEVER.

230

YOU DID IT!

You turned the page! You finished the book! Welcome to the Spell/Sword fandom. Wait, don't give me that look, this is a big deal. A HUGE deal. Or rather, it will be. Maybe?

This book is self-published. Which means that it hasn't been sanctioned by a copy editor, or traditional publisher, and it's not remotely marketable to the populace at large.

It also means I work for you. That's what I want, that's all I've ever wanted. You've already done more for me than I could ever dream – just by reading the book.

But now I need more.

I need your help.

I need you to get people to read the book.

Sing to them. Bake exotic muffinry and treats. Lie to them. And thus the fandom will grow through deceit and manipulation.

I have a story to tell you – a long story that ends in shadow. I need you to help me trick other people into reading it.

You were here first, you got on board with the Swordpunk Movement on the ground floor.

And when we're rioting in the streets, drinking hot mead from the skulls of our oppressors – I will wipe my mouth with the ornate purple cape that I am wearing, and pin the Star of Literary Violence upon your chest. I'll probably accidentally stick you a little bit, but please know that it's just my pride in our success that is making my hands shake, and not this rancid mead that you fermented in an empty Coke machine.

It will be a beautiful moment, no?

Sic Semper Tyrannosaur,
G. Derek Adams
spell-sword.com